SPECIAL MESSAGE TO READERS

This book is published under the auspices of

THE ULVERSCROFT FOUNDATION

(registered charity No. 264873 UK)

Established in 1972 to provide funds for research, diagnosis and treatment of eye diseases. Examples of contributions made are: —

A Children's Assessment Unit at Moorfield's Hospital, London.

•

Twin operating theatres at the Western Ophthalmic Hospital, London.

•

A Chair of Ophthalmology at the Royal Australian College of Ophthalmologists.

•

The Ulverscroft Children's Eye Unit at the Great Ormond Street Hospital For Sick Children, London.

You can help further the work of the Foundation by making a donation or leaving a legacy. Every contribution, no matter how small, is received with gratitude. Please write for details to:

THE ULVERSCROFT FOUNDATION,
The Green, Bradgate Road, Anstey,
Leicester LE7 7FU, England.
Telephone: (0116) 236 4325

In Australia write to:
THE ULVERSCROFT FOUNDATION,
c/o The Royal Australian and New Zealand College of Ophthalmologists,
94-98, Chalmers Street, Surry Hills,
N.S.W. 2010, Australia

HER RELUCTANT HEART

Danielle Cachart is looking forward to spending the summer on the French Ile d'Oléron . . . with maybe a little romance thrown in for good measure. When fate flings her into the life of Alex Gallepe and his young son, Christian, Dani finds herself facing danger on two fronts — the literal danger of armed bank robbers . . . and the emotional danger of falling in love with Christian's widowed father. But is Dani prepared to face the commitment required?

Books by Karen Abbott
in the Linford Romance Library:

RED ROSE GIRL
SUMMER ISLAND
A TIME TO FORGIVE
LOVE IS BLIND
LOVE CONQUERS ALL
A MATTER OF TRUST
DESIGNS FOR LOVE
WHEN TRUE LOVE WINS
A TASTE OF HAPPINESS
THE HEART KNOWS NO BOUNDS
THE TURNING TIDE
OUTRAGEOUS DECEPTION
RISING TO THE CALL
A FRENCH MASQUERADE
A HEART DIVIDED
DANGER COMES CALLING
TO FACE THE PAST
DANGEROUS INTRIGUE
JUST A SUMMER ROMANCE
AN UNSUITABLE ALLIANCE

KAREN ABBOTT

HER RELUCTANT HEART

Complete and Unabridged

LINFORD
Leicester

First published in Great Britain in 2005

First Linford Edition
published 2006

British Library CIP Data

Abbott, Karen
Her reluctant heart.—Large print ed.—
Linford romance library
1. Love stories
2. Large type books
I. Title
823.9′14 [F]

ISBN 1–84617–336–1

Published by
F. A. Thorpe (Publishing)
Anstey, Leicestershire

Set by Words & Graphics Ltd.
Anstey, Leicestershire
Printed and bound in Great Britain by
T. J. International Ltd., Padstow, Cornwall

This book is printed on acid-free paper

1

Danielle Cachart smiled in delight as she stepped down from the long Charente Maritime bus on the outskirts of the small town of Le Château on Ile d'Oléron. She knew she'd been right to come!

The idea had formed whilst reading the long chatty letter from her friend, Lys Dupont, who had had to pull out of their shared plans to have a 'working' summer holiday somewhere in the vicinity of the Mediterranean, and had come instead to look after her elderly grandfather who lived in an old windmill on Ile d'Oléron.

After a few lonely weeks spent with her uncle, Dani had impulsively decided to join her and, if the heat and glare of the afternoon sun that was bearing down upon her was anything to go by, this wasn't the poorer option!

The bus pulled away, leaving Dani facing, across the road, the back of the local Tourist Information Office. Beyond that was the spacious town square, bordered by Les Halles du Marché and numerous shops, cafés and a couple of hotels.

Gaily coloured bunting stretched from branch to branch of the trees around the square and the air was filled with the sound of music, laughter and the constant buzz of human voices, all of which proclaimed to Dani that the usually quiet town that Lys had described in her letter, was enjoying its annual influx of holiday makers and all that that entailed.

Dani grinned in delight. With all these visitors on the island, there'd be no shortage of summer jobs. If Lys couldn't suggest any employment near to where she was now living with her grandfather, Dani would lose no time in finding a suitable job around here.

First things first though — seek out a bus timetable, to enable her to continue her journey to Le Deu, a small village farther up the island near Vertbois, a small coastal village where, according to Lys, the Atlantic surf surged onto the beach with relentless force.

Her enquiries in the tourist office gave her the news that there was only one more bus that day and it would leave the stand at eighteen hundred hours. Undaunted, Dani asked for permission to leave her large rucksack in a safe corner and then re-emerged into the brilliant sunshine to join the masses. She could already feel the holiday spirit invading her. She had four hours to fill.

After buying an ice-cream from a pavement vendor, Dani strolled round the square among the other holiday-makers, drinking in the atmosphere and enjoying the live music being provided by individual musicians . . . a violinist rendering a lively tune standing in the shade of a leafy tree, a flautist fingering a haunting melody over by the fountain, and an accordion player surrounded by a group of dancers in colourful dress on the grass by the tourist office.

A temporary stage had been set up at one end of the square. A lively sketch was just finishing and a voice over a loudspeaker announced that the Carnival Parade was approaching the square from the direction of the citadel.

Dani found herself caught up in the surge of movement of the crowd and was in time to see the start of the procession emerge from the road opposite the square. It was led by a number of musicians and local dignitaries ensconced in a motorised tourist train that proclaimed itself to be Le Petit Train.

Twenty or so garishly-dressed clowns accompanied the procession, some carrying buckets to collect donations from the crowd and others cavorting and tumbling alongside, occasionally diving amongst the crowded spectators to temporarily involve them in their activity.

Dani's hands were seized by a clown wearing a curly orange wig and dressed in a baggy white all-in-one suit with multi-coloured pompom balls sewn down the front. His face was suitably painted in the traditional clown guise and only his eyes remained his own. They were as dark as ebony and dancing with laughter and Dani responded immediately, surrendering to the unspoken invitation to join in the spontaneous lively caper along the street.

Only when she was eventually completely out of breath did she laughingly plead for release and regretfully let him go on his way, which he did with a seeming rueful glance of his own as he waved a hand in farewell.

Many of the crowd were moving on with the procession and Dani followed suit, laughing and waving in response to participants in the procession.

Out beyond the confines of the town wall, she realised that they were on the road to the port, which then led to the viaduct that linked the island to the mainland. It was out of her way, away from the bus departure point and when she spotted a small café on the corner of the road, she decided instead that it was time for a cool drink.

A tall glass of raspberry milk-shake was very refreshing and a Viennese pastry took the edge off her appetite. A glance at her watch revealed that it was still only half-past four, leaving an hour-and-a-half until the time of her bus departure . . . and she wondered for the first time if turning up unannounced, as a surprise for her friend, had been such a good idea. Maybe she should telephone Lys and warn her of her arrival?

She reached into her shoulder bag for her mobile phone, frowning at the information on its small screen. The lack of ascending red lines at its right-hand edge showed that she had forgotten to recharge the battery before starting on her journey.

That meant a public call-box. She remembered seeing one outside the post office on the corner of the square and was about to retrace her steps along the road, when the sight of a young boy standing alone caught her attention. She guessed he was about four years old and she could see that he was close to tears but was manfully fighting them. The need for a phone box forgotten, Dani hesitantly approached him and crouched down in front of him.

'Hello! Have you lost your mummy?'

'No,' he hiccupped. 'I've lost Brigitte.'

His lower lip wobbled and he woefully looked all around, searching for the familiar figure. Dani squatted beside him, aware as she did so that a child's view was limited by lack of height. All he could see was a medley of bodies passing by.

'Who is Brigitte? Your sister?' Dani asked, glancing around, hoping to see an older girl who might be anxiously searching for her little brother.

'No! Silly!' the boy said scathingly. 'Brigitte's my childminder! She told me to stay on the swing . . . but she was busy talking on her phone to Rodrigue, and I wanted to find my daddy. So I ran away! Only, now . . . '

His dark eyes looked around anxiously, ' . . . I can't find my way back.'

'Oh, dear! And I'm new here. I don't know where the swings are.'

'We could look for them,' the boy suggested, looking hopefully at her.

'You're quite right!' Dani agreed, thankful to see him looking more cheerful. 'What's your name? I'm called Dani.'

'My name is Christian Alexandré Gallepe,' the boy recited seriously. 'But I can't tell you where we live because we haven't lived here long and I haven't had time to learn my address yet.'

'Right, Christian, I think we had better find out where the swings are and see if Brigitte is there looking for you . . . and, if we have no luck there, I will have to take you to the gendarmerie because . . . '

A sharp report, followed by a series of shouts from across the road interrupted her words and she instinctively drew Christian closer to her as she rose to her feet and stretched her neck to see what was happening.

'It was probably a firework,' she murmured, hoping to reassure the young boy, seeing his eyes stretch wide with apprehension.

She could see a mêlée of confusion outside the opposite building, which she now realised was a bank. Two figures dressed in clown outfits who were running out of the door seemed to be the cause of the incident, and Dani wondered why the few pedestrians who were nearer to them than she was didn't try to stop them. It was only when one of them paused to look over his shoulder and raised his arm, followed by another sharp report, that Dani realised that the clowns were armed with guns . . . and using them.

'Oh, my goodness!' she exclaimed, pulling Christian once more into the shelter of her body. She instinctively thought of the clown who had drawn her into his mad caper along the street

. . . and thrust from her mind the thought that one of the clowns in the incident might be him.

No. Surely he had been too carefree to have been biding his time before robbing a bank. Or was he a hardened criminal and it was all part of a well-practised plan? She didn't know. How could she?

'There's my daddy!' Christian called, struggling to free himself.

'What? Where?'

Distracted by Christian's voice, Dani looked around but her attention was seized by two motorbikes roaring out of the car park behind the bank. They pulled up by the clowns, lingering only until they had clambered aboard and then roared towards the corner of the road when Dani stood immobile, her arms gripping hold of Christian.

Her feet felt rooted to the ground and, for a frightening moment, she thought the leading motorbike was going to run straight into them. A surge of adrenalin enabled her to swoop the boy into her arms and swing her body round, away from its path and, to her immense relief, the two bikes roared down the road towards the viaduct.

Her legs were shaking and she lowered the boy to the ground, oblivious to the people now rushing past her to get to the scene of the crime across the road. She subconsciously heard the sound of police sirens and saw uniformed figures running into the bank and was vaguely aware that at least two police vehicles had gone in pursuit of the motorbikes . . . but her main attention was on the boy at her side.

'I saw my daddy!' he said again.

Dani dropped down to his height. 'Where did you see him?' she asked, looking around to see if she could see a man who might possibly be Christian's father . . . but no-one seemed to fit the picture. 'Can you see him now?'

'No, he's gone now,' Christian replied. 'I expect he didn't see me. Did you see the clown with orange hair?' he added eagerly.

Dani shook her head. All she had seen were the two clowns . . . and she realised why they had chosen that particular disguise on this particular day. That was all most people would see and remember . . . two clowns, dressed practically identical to about two dozen other clowns who had frolicked around the town that afternoon.

'There were lots of clowns in town today,' she mused quietly. 'The bank robbers must have known that. Oh, look!'

A cavalcade of police vehicles arrived at the scene, their sirens blaring. Moves were made to cordon off the bank and keep the steady influx of goggle-eyed spectators at bay and Dani retreated with the rest.

She heard a request that any witnesses with any relevant first-hand information should make themselves known in order to make a statement but it seemed more pressing to find Christian's childminder than to register her less than reliable eye-witness account.

Christian would make a better witness than she would . . . and, from the number of volunteers making their way over to the uniformed officer, they had plenty of others ready to testify.

'I think we'd better try to find Brigitte,' she suggested. 'She'll be out of her mind with worry.' She took hold of his hand. 'Come on, let's ask someone where the swings are.'

The second person she asked suggested she try a small playground that was just a few hundred metres down the next road by the post office, so they set off up the slight rise that led back into the old walled town. Just through two tall stone pillars that had stood beside the ancient town gates Dani paused momentarily.

She could see the gendarmerie across the road. A harassed-looking gendarme was rushing down the steps and Dani could imagine the scene inside. No-one would welcome the added problem of a lost child, especially if he could be reunited without any fuss with Brigitte at the playground.

Christian tugged at her hand.

'I came down that road,' he said pointing ahead. 'I remember it now.'

He walked with Dani to where the post office stood just beyond a set of traffic lights. A signpost on the corner indicated that the road led to the ancient fortified citadel and the small playground was partway down the road. A number of small children were playing, watched over by an assortment of people . . . parents, grandparents and such . . . but no-one who seemed as if she were frantically looking for her charge.

'Is Brigitte here?' Dani asked Christian.

'No.'

Dani sighed. If the girl was anxiously searching the surrounding area, there was no knowing where her search might have led her.

'Oh, well, it looks like it will have to be the gendarmerie . . . if they have anyone to spare.' She squeezed Christian's hand reassuringly. 'Come on!

Back we go. We passed it on our way here.'

'Has Brigitte got lost, too?' Christian asked, as they crossed over the road.

'It seems so,' Dani replied, 'but I wouldn't worry too much about her. I'm sure she'll be able to find her way home . . . or even to the gendarmerie, which is where we're going now. Uh-Oh!'

The added exclamation was caused by the sight of a police car swerving recklessly through the traffic lights by the post office, its lights blazing and heading straight for her and Christian. For the second time that day, she clutched hold of Christian and pulled him close, though it was only a reflex action. Her worry, this time, wasn't that they were about to be mown down by reckless driving!

Barely had the car drawn level when a man tumbled out of the passenger seat, causing her to step back a pace. Even so, he almost knocked her over as he swooped upon Christian and swept him up into his arms.

Only then did he turn towards Dani with ice-cold eyes.

'How dare you try to abduct my son?'

2

'Abduct your son!' Dani echoed in disbelief. 'How dare you! I think you rather ought to reconsider your choice of childminder who finds herself too busy talking to keep a watchful eye on her charge!'

Furiously, she looked him straight in the eyes. The coldness there pierced her heart, but, as their eyes held, a momentary glimmer of 'something', she wasn't sure what, lightened the freezing depths — but it vanished as swiftly as it had appeared and she wondered later if she had imagined it.

She tried to step away but an iron fist clamped itself around her wrist and held her fast.

'Leave my choice of childminder out of this!' the man said fiercely. 'It is your actions that we are concerned about. You were seen, with my son, walking up the hill past the gendarmerie not ten minutes ago. If you had no evil intent, you would have taken Christian straight there!'

'Evil intent?'

Her mind froze in horror at the word. Dumbfounded, she blurted out, 'I had no evil intent. Everyone was busy with the aftermath of the bank raid. It seemed simpler to bring Christian back to the playground to see if Brigitte were still here.'

'Ha! You admit removing him from the playground, then?'

'No!'

She was aware that the scene was attracting the beginnings of an audience and she sighed in defeat, her fury at his accusation slipping away. He had been frightened by Christian's absence. Any father would be. He had lashed out in anger.

'Look, there's no need for this,' she pleaded. 'I can explain what happened. Christian was lost. I didn't see him until I got up to leave the café opposite the bank. I was helping him, not abducting him.'

Her hand had instinctively gestured towards the child, whose face was buried in his father's shoulder but Gallepe twisted his body as if her contact with his son would inflict a plague upon him.

'Do not touch my son.'

Dani felt her face blanch and she stepped back as if lashed.

'But, Papa!' the small boy objected, twisting in his father's arms to regard his face.

Dani felt a hand grip hold of her shoulder. It was the driver of the police car.

'I'll take over now, monsieur!' he said grimly. 'Get into the car, mademoiselle.'

Dani felt a wash of shame flow over her as she stooped to get into the rear of the police car and was thankful that no-one in the crowd knew her.

She cast a backward glance through the rear window and could see Gallepe holding the hand of his small son as they followed them down the road. In spite of the injustice Dani felt, she knew the man was overwrought and just needed time to calm down. She hoped Christian was telling his father what had really happened.

By the time Christian and his father reached the gendarmerie, Dani had been released from the rear of the car and hustled through the outer reception area into a room towards the rear. She was cautioned and offered the services of a lawyer but she declined the offer. It would take extra time and a glance at the clock on the wall made her hope that everything would be sorted out without too much of a delay . . . or she would be stranded here overnight.

Dani was partway through her explanation when a knock on the door heralded the arrival of Gallepe. One look at his face showed that Christian had indeed told his father how he had wandered away from the playground and Dani wondered how gracious his father's apology would be.

'It seems we acted precipitously, mademoiselle,' Gallepe ventured, after a few words with her interrogator. 'Though I must point out that you acted very foolishly by not bringing Christian directly here.'

'Yes, I'm sorry,' she excused herself. 'I just thought that, if Brigitte were still at the playground looking for Christian, it would be better to simply reunite them.'

After a few formalities, Dani was given permission to leave the gendarmerie without any further action to be taken, but was given a repeat of Gallepe's criticism of her action. Dani accepted the rebuke.

'Has Brigitte shown up yet?' she asked conversationally, as she accompanied Gallepe and Christian outside. She felt a wave of freedom wash over her, making her feel a little light-headed.

'No, and she will have some explaining to do, when she does so!' Gallepe said grimly. He held out his hand. 'Once again, I ask your forgiveness for my rash accusation, mademoiselle. I can only plead the anxiety I had over Christian's safety.'

Dani took hold of his hand. It felt cool and firm, a bit like his character, she reflected.

'That's all right. I understand,' she replied with a smile.

She let go of his hand and crouched down in front of Christian.

'And always stay with your childminder, Christian,' she advised him. 'Then you won't get lost again.'

Christian nodded, his head down.

'What are you going to say to Mademoiselle Cachart, Christian?' his father reminded him sternly.

Dani glanced up at him as he spoke and was startled to see that, in spite of his sternness, there was a gentleness about his face now and she wondered that she hadn't noticed it before.

'I'm sorry,' Christian mumbled, scuffling the toes of his shoes on the pavement.

'And?' prompted his father patiently.

Whilst his attention was on his son, Dani scrutinised his face. He was darkly tanned, suggesting that he worked outdoors, though his hands were suggesting that his work wasn't manual. He was very good-looking, with his dark hair cut reasonably short and brushed back off his face.

'Thank you for looking after me,' Christian's small voice cut into her thoughts.

'That's all right. It was my pleasure,' Dani answered softly, gently squeezing his shoulders. She straightened up and faced his father, now noting his firm chin and the suggestion of a dimple at the corner of his mouth. His lips were forming into a farewell smile and Dani felt her heart begin to flip as the warmth of his smile enveloped her.

Careful! This man is married, with a young son. Hands off!

'If you'll excuse me, Monsieur Gallepe, I must go. I have a bus to catch,' she added, looking at her watch.

‘Oh, no!’ The dismay in her voice was unmistakable.

‘There is a problem, mademoiselle?’

‘My bus has gone, and I bet the tourist information is closed, too! I left my bag there,’ she added by the way of explanation.

All romantic notions flew out of her head and practicality took over. She thrust out her hand once more in a farewell gesture. ‘I’m sorry, Monsieur Gallepe, I must go. I need to telephone my friend and let her know I’m here. I’m sure she’ll come out to pick me up.’

Gallepe held on to her hand. ‘You are staying on the island?’

‘Yes. That is, hopefully! I’ve come unannounced, to surprise my friend! She lives at Le Deu, a small village near Vertbois. That’s on the Atlantic coast . . . ’

‘I know where it is, mademoiselle. We are staying at Vertbois ourselves. You must allow me to take you to your friend’s home. It’s the least I can do after all this,’ waving his hand towards the gendarmerie.

Her hand was still trapped in his and Dani was aware of all sorts of tingles coursing through her.

'Is Dani coming to our house?' Christian asked.

'Not quite,' his father smiled, 'but maybe she will another day, if that's possible.'

He looked enquiringly at Dani but Dani didn't want to commit herself.

She wasn't sure she could cope with a friendship with a married man, even if the friendship had been brought about by his young son.

'I'll see,' she temporised. 'I'm hoping to get a job for the summer, so I expect that will keep me quite busy.'

They set off to walk to the car park near the citadel, where Gallepe had parked his car earlier in the afternoon. As they turned into the road they could see the figure of a young teenager hovering uncertainly at the top of the steps at the entrance to the playground, anxiously looking up and down the road.

Dani wasn't surprised when Christian said, 'There's Brigitte!'

'So I see,' his father said grimly. He rooted in his trouser pocket for his car keys and handed them to Dani. 'Take Christian to my car, will you, Dani. He'll show you which one it is. Press this button to turn off the alarm.'

A bemused Dani did as she was bidden and, after fastening Christian into his car seat, she seated herself beside him. Having already been on the receiving end of his anger, she didn't envy Brigitte her turn, even though it was more deserved than her own.

It was five minutes before Christian's father escorted the subdued teenager to the car and opened the rear door of the silver open-topped Peugeot.

'Join me in the front, please, Mademoiselle Cachart, if you will? Brigitte will sit with Christian.'

There was a strained atmosphere throughout the journey that only Christian seemed to be unaware of . . . and he only chattered briefly before falling asleep in his car seat, emotionally worn out by his unscheduled adventure.

'Where is your friend's home, mademoiselle?' Gallepe asked as they drew near to Le Deu.

'I'm not sure,' Dani admitted, 'but it's next to a windmill.'

'Ah! I knew it. We are almost there.'

Round a bend in the road . . . and there it was. Scaffolding had been erected around the outside of the windmill and it was in the process of being repainted.

A single-storey cottage stood about a hundred metres away. Hollyhocks grew profusely against its sunny wall and rambling roses twined themselves around an old-fashioned well in the courtyard.

Dani turned to Christian's father. 'Thank you for the lift, Monsieur Gallepe.'

'Call me Alex,' he smiled. 'I'm sure we'll meet again.'

'Yes,' Dani responded noncommittally as she slid out of her seat, doubting the wisdom of his intention.

She smiled briefly at the still discomfited Brigitte and pushed the door closed.

With a wave of his hand and a devastating smile that made Dani even less sure of his wisdom in expecting any sort of casual friendship between them, Alex drove on his way.

Dani watched until the car was out of sight and then turned towards the windmill. What would Lys say when she saw her?

'Dani!'

Lys's shriek nearly lifted the roof off the small stone cottage. She hesitated in disbelief for only a second or two before she flung her wide arms and ran towards the doorway where Dani stood framed against the outside brightness.

Dani let go of her apprehension about the reception of her unannounced visit and met her friend's undoubted welcome with as loud a squeal of her own. They hugged, held each other at arm's length and hugged again.

'You sly puss!' Lys teasingly accused Dani. 'Why didn't you let me know you were coming? I'd have met you in Le Château!'

Her eyes narrowed slightly, as her brain slipped into gear. 'How did you get here, by the way? The bus went by ages since, just before I stopped work.' She indicated her paint-splattered hands that she had been in the process of washing.

Dani laughed. 'It's a long story, though I'm sure you'll enjoy it. The thing is, I'm rather hoping I'll be able to stay with you for a while. What d'you think? I'll get a job of some sort. I'll pay my way.'

'Goose! As if that matters! 'Course you can stay. I'm sure Grandpère will make no objection. He's not exactly living here himself, at the moment. We had a bit of bother with someone breaking in and turning the place over a few weeks ago and he's been staying at a neighbour's house ever since. You remember he'd had a heart attack, don't you?'

Dani did remember. It was that fact

that had shattered their plans to spend the summer together . . . and led Lys and her grandfather to consider renovating the long-disused windmill into a working museum for people to visit.

A charcoal line-drawing of an elderly man was displayed on the old dresser which stood along an inner wall.

'Is that your grandfather, Lys? Has Xavier drawn it?'

'Yes. Wait 'til you meet Grandpère and you see how lifelike it is! Xavier has a wonderful talent. He'll be famous one day, you wait and see. He's very popular with the tourists. He had some gorgeous paintings of some horses when he first arrived here but they were stolen one night and he got pretty well knocked about by the thieves.'

'Didn't you say his father is a Count?'

'Yes, but they've hit a rough time recently and he obviously needs to work for his living. He runs a racing stable and stud farm and Xavier did the paintings on commission for some of the owners. The loss of the money was quite a blow to him.'

'What's the Count like? Did you have to curtsey when you met him?'

'Of course not! He's not royalty. He's just an ordinary man. Mind you, he did arrive in his own helicopter, so I suppose they must be above averagely rich. But Xavier's the younger son. He's got to make his own way in life. None of the inheritance will come to him. It will all go to his brother. In fact, he thought his brother was mixed up in the theft of his painting, but Henri swears he wasn't!'

'Some brother! Still, you can't chose your relations, can you?'

Dani grinned at Lys.

'Anyway, I can't wait to meet Xavier! D'you think he'll do my portrait?'

'Probably. Just join the queue. He has a studio in an old fisherman's hut near the port at Le Château. He'll sketch a quick likeness for five euros! You'd better get in quick before he puts his prices up to reflect his true worth.

'I'll do that! Anyway, enough about your boyfriend. Wait 'til I tell you what happened to me this afternoon. I got myself arrested, no less!'

Dani light-heartedly shared the events that had happened since she set foot on the island, raising incredible laughter and teasing remarks from Lys until they were giggling like a pair of schoolgirls after a telling-off from their senior mistress.

When they had sobered sufficiently, Lys took her along to meet her grandpère, who was living temporarily with Madame Giraud, the local patisserie owner. Madame Giraud had made a large enough quantity of food for their evening meal to stretch to include Dani and afterwards Lys insisted that she went with her back to Le Château to spend the evening with Xavier and the other artisans who were renting similar studios to Xavier's near the port.

The small commune of simple wooden studios had originally been the working cabins of some of the many fishermen of Ile d'Oléron, whose trade, though still in existence, was not as prolific as in former years.

It was a wonderful introduction to the island's nightlife. They were a good-natured crowd and Dani light-heartedly fended off much flirtatious banter offered by some of the young artisans.

It had been a long day and Dani was glad when Lys suggested that they made for home. Sleep wasn't long in settling upon her and, in the morning, Dani was disconcerted to realise that her dreams had been peppered with the elusive memory of a pair of shining ebony eyes, but she found it impossible to decide whether they belonged to her dashing, frolicking clown, or to Christian's handsome father.

3

Alex spent the early part of the evening playing with Christian, allowing him to talk about his afternoon adventure and his curiosity about the clowns playing at 'bang-bangs'.

'Was it like when they are in the circus, falling off their bikes and throwing buckets of water at everyone? Christian asked anxiously. 'And one always runs away pretending to be frightened?'

'Something like that,' Alex replied tentatively, trying to find a middle course between warning of the danger but not making his son more upset than was necessary. 'But it was wrong to frighten people who didn't know it was a game. Some people found it very alarming. And it is always wrong to steal money.'

'Were the clowns bad, then, Papa?'

'Those particular ones were. They weren't real clowns, you see.'

Christian swept into his arms and swinging him around with his legs flying out.

'I was a bit naughty, though, wasn't I?'

'You mean leaving Brigitte like that? Yes, you were. I hope you'll never do anything like that again.'

'I'm sorry, Papa,' Christian said in a subdued voice. His face brightened. 'But I did meet Dani, didn't I? She bought me an ice-cream and found the swings again. You weren't really cross with her, were you?'

'Only at first, because I thought she had taken you away from Brigitte.'

'That was silly, Papa! She wouldn't do that! She's nice. I knew that straight away.'

Alex was bemused by Christian's uncomplicated instant character assessment, but he nodded his head. 'Yes, she's nice.'

The memory of his outburst and hasty accusation brought a wry twist to his lips. She probably didn't think he was very nice. The thought startled him and unaccountably subdued him for the remainder of the evening.

The first thing the two girls did the next day was to inspect the interior of the windmill. Lys described with pride how dilapidated it had been less than two months previously and how they had achieved its swift renovation.

'We got a grant from the local council because it is hoped to draw tourists into the area,' she explained as she opened the solid wooden door and ushered Dani inside. 'And because we are doing some of the work ourselves, we have been able to engage a specialist to renovate the sails and all the machinery.'

Dani was impressed and she could tell that Lys was full of enthusiasm for the renovating scheme.

'And what will you do when it's all up and running?' she asked. 'Will you still live here with your grandfather and help him to run the place?'

‘Certainly at first, then I’ll have to see how things go.’

‘Like how things progress between you and Xavier,’ Dani ventured, her eyes smiling.

Lys met her gaze frankly. ‘I know we haven’t known each other for very long, but we seem to feel the same way about each other. I think we’ll make a go of it.’

Her face glowed as she spoke of Xavier and Dani knew that her friend was very much in love.

‘And we have the rest of the summer in front of us before we need to make any permanent decisions,’ Lys continued. ‘Xavier wants to make as much use of his time on Ile d’Oléron to fire his imagination through the winter months, when he will probably return to Paris to work, and I want to get this project up and running for Grandpère.

‘After that, it should make enough profit for him to employ a couple of part-time workers. It’s giving him an incentive to get fully strong again, which was missing before, and it's made me realise that I can get to grips with a project and make it work. I didn't know where I was going before. What about you? Have you thought about what direction you want to go in?'

Dani shook her head. 'Not really. You never know, the island might have something to show me, too.'

They emerged into the brilliant sunshine, just as a car drew up on the land that was to become their car park.

'Hmm, who's this dishy fellow?' Lys wondered aloud, as the driver stepped out of his car.

'Oh!' Dani blushed. 'It's Alex. You know, Christian's father, whom I told you about yesterday. I wonder what he wants?'

'You, by the look of it.' Lys grinned. 'Isn't he married, though?'

'Mmm, it would seem so.' Dani sighed. 'Aren't all the best ones?'

However, she smiled at Alex as he walked towards her. 'Bonjour, Dani!' he greeted her warmly, his glance sweeping on to Lys and including her, as he murmured, 'Mademoiselle.'

'This is my friend, Lys,' Dani introduced her, repeating Alex's name to Lys. 'Lys was showing me the work she's done on the windmill.'

'You'll have to come when it's finished and bring Christian,' Lys invited, adding with wide-eyed innocence, 'and anyone else in your family.'

Alex merely smiled his pleasure. 'Thank you, mademoiselle. Christian will enjoy that. In fact, I didn't dare tell him I was coming this way today, as I knew he would pester me to bring him and I didn't know if it would be convenient.'

He turned to Dani and smiled disarmingly. 'I have to go to Le Château and wondered if you had made arrangements to collect your luggage from the tourist information office. If not, I will be pleased to offer you a lift, to make up in some measure for my unmerited accusation yesterday.'

Dani, aware of the rapid beating of her heart and the delicious churning of her stomach as she took the full force of Alex's devastating smile, wondered if it would be more prudent to say that other arrangements had been made. She reflected wryly that a married man ought to show more reserve about where he directed such a heart-disturbing smile.

He hadn't denied his married state, she had noticed sadly that he had merely ignored Lys's probe. Before she could speak, however, Lys once more took a hand in the proceedings.

'What a good idea!' she exclaimed brightly. 'That means I can get to work as soon as René arrives. We're hoping to finish painting the mill today and the cottage tomorrow.'

'Is that a 'yes'?' Alex smiled.

'I guess so.' Dani smiled back, assuring herself that there was no harm in accepting a lift into town with Alex, married or not. 'I'll help you as soon as I get back, Lys,' Dani promised.

Seated at Alex's side, the wind whipping back her long hair, Dani found herself gradually relaxing. Alex's dark eyes seemed full of warmth today and his glance gave no trace of apology or guilt for inviting her company.

'Are you married?' Dani heard herself blurt out without having meant to do so. Heavens! How gauche it made her seem!

Alex smiled. 'Would it make any difference?'

Dani felt her cheeks flood with heat. 'Not for an outing such as this. I just wondered, that's all. You haven't mentioned a wife.'

'In spite of your friend's attempt to entice the information out of me?'

'Did you mind?'

He grinned. 'Not at all. That's what friends are for!'

They were at a crossroad and he turned to face her as he pulled on the handbrake. 'The answer is, no, I haven't a wife. Sadly, she died nearly a year ago. A horse she was riding bolted and threw her. She broke her neck and died instantly.'

His face lost its glow as he spoke and Dani could see traces of the agony he must have suffered.

'I'm sorry,' she said softly. 'You must miss her dreadfully, and Christian.'

'Yes, it's been a hard year. Christian hardly remembers her now, of course. As for me, I feel I'm just emerging from a dark tunnel. I expect things will be easier when Christian starts school. I had to place him in a nursery school but it's closed now, until September.'

'Hence Brigitte?'

He laughed ruefully. 'As you say, 'Hence Brigitte'! Not one of my better decisions, it seems.'

'She'll learn.'

'I'm not so sure, I've left Christian with a more elderly neighbour today, a Madame Toussaint.'

'At least she won't be talking on the phone to her boyfriend.'

Alex laughed. 'There is that advantage, I suppose. I'm more worried that she'll just fall asleep or forget about him.'

It wasn't easy for him, Dani reflected, wondering how involved she wanted to be with a man who had a four-year-old boy to care for. He was attractive and she liked him, but did she want to be a surrogate childminder?

'Do you live here?' she asked, breaking a companionable silence.

'Only for the summer. It seemed better to come to a place like this, than to try to keep Christian amused in our home in Paris.'

'You must have an amenable job,' Dani marvelled, 'or are you in education, and thus free for the summer?'

'That's a thought, but, no. I manage an international team of salesmen. I can work just as well on my home computer linked to the internet as I can at head office. It's very flexible, so I generally manage quite well. And you? What do you generally do?'

'Oh, nothing much, yet. I've just left university and hoped to get a summer job somewhere in Italy with Lys, until her grandfather took ill. I'm going to look for something to do here, if I can, then I can spend some time with Lys. I'm sure I'll get something.'

They were approaching the town now and Alex drove towards the market square. He glanced at his watch.

'My business should take me until about twelve-thirty. I don't think there's a bus back before two o'clock, so if you'd like to spend time looking around, how about us meeting for lunch at the Hotel Paris over there and I'll then take you home again, unless there's anything else you'd rather do?'

'No, that will do fine,' Dani assured him.

She decided to check that it was all right to leave her bag a while longer at the tourist information office and then approach various hotels and bars to see if there was any chance of temporary work. This she did and, to her disappointment, nothing suitable was offered to her. With the season already underway, places were taken and only the more menial sort of jobs needed replacements.

Just before half-past-twelve, as she was crossing the market square, Dani heard her name called. Turning round, she was pleased to see Xavier Monsigny hailing her with a radiant smile. Son of a Count or not, he looked the typical artisan with his dark brown hair fastened in dreadlocks and held back from his head with a braided band. He was pleasant to talk to and Dani repeated her request for a sketched portrait at some time.

'But, of course,' he promised. 'I can do it now, if you would like.'

Dani glanced at her watch. 'I'm sorry,' she said regretfully. 'I have a lunch date at half-past. I'm almost late, as it is.'

'Then, some other time. You know where my studio is, or I can do it the next time I come to the windmill.'

He smiled again and Dani could see why Lys was so captivated by him. He had the ability to make each person feel they were the whole centre of his attention. His artistic eye, no doubt.

With a few more pleasantries, they said goodbye and Dani hurried in the direction of the hotel that Alex had pointed out to her. Ah, there he was, waiting for her by the far exit. She waved and he returned the salute.

'Well met!' She smiled, aware that her legs were trembling.

'Then I am here just in time,' He smiled back. He glanced back across the square. 'Do you know that young man you were talking to?'

'Who? Oh, Xavier? Yes, he's Lys's boyfriend, you know, the artist I told you about. Why? Do you know him?'

There was a fractional hesitation before Alex shook his head. 'I don't think so. He just reminded me of someone. No matter! Come! Let's go to lunch.'

He was the perfect host, suggesting choices from the excellent menu and choosing the best wine to accompany their choice.

'You've been here before,' Dani challenged with a smile, after noticing the ease of familiarity from the waiter towards Alex.

Alex nodded. 'I always find it preferable to remain loyal to a select number of restaurants, especially when I have a guest with me. There's nothing worse than finding a place isn't up to standard.'

'You needn't worry with me.' She laughed. 'Cheap pavement cafés were our idea of a good meal out when we were students. I bet your eating places in Paris differ from mine.'

'Then, you must introduce me to them some time.' He smiled.

Dani wondered how definitely he meant that but decided not to make an issue of it, still unsure about getting any closer to him.

As they walked back to Alex's car, Dani wondered if Alex would try to make arrangements to see her again, but he didn't. Whether she was sorry or relieved, she wasn't quite sure. How typical, she thought, not to be given the chance to exercise her better judgement and refuse to get further involved.

It was just after two o'clock when he dropped her off outside the mill and, with a cheery wave of his hand, drove away.

Lys was eager to learn how she had fared in her job-hunting and, surprisingly, wasn't as disappointed as she was.

'In fact, it's quite convenient, really,' Lys commented after listening to Dani's woeful tale of failure to obtain some form of work.

'What d'you mean?' Dani asked her friend, curiously.

'I was talking things over with Grandpère this morning, after you had gone and he suggested that you help us out here,' Lys told her. 'The sooner we are up and running the better, and we have all the publicity to get ready. I don't really want to leave it all to outsiders and I know you have a leaning towards that sort of thing. Xavier has drawn some sketches that I want to use and, between us, I'm sure we can come up with the proper wording. What do you think?'

'I think it's wonderful!' Dani exclaimed. 'When do we begin?'

'Right now, if you want to.' Lys laughed. 'René said he'll do the preparation on the outside of the cottage, if we will finish the windmill. So, come on! There's a pair of overalls and a spare paintbrush. Let's show that boyfriend of mine that others besides himself are good at painting!'

4

In the next two days, Dani and Lys made great progress painting the remainder of the exterior of the windmill and the cottage.

'Even the cottage would be a tourist attraction,' Dani remarked, as they stepped back to admire their work. 'It wouldn't take much to put it back as it was a hundred years ago.'

'Is that the polite way of saying we're living in a hovel?' Lys asked in mock severity.

Dani grinned. 'No, but your grandfather hasn't exactly moved with the times, has he?'

'You can say that again! It's not so bad in the summer but I'm sure it must get pretty cold in the winter and there's only the stove to keep the place warm.'

'Your grandfather could lock his bedroom door and put the rest of the cottage on show, a bit like the nobility opening up their châteaux . . . ' Dani continued, enthusiastically warming to her scheme. ' . . . and Madame Giraud could have bread or something baking in the oven. Then, everyone would want to buy some and forget all about the supermarket bread, no matter how much cheaper it is to buy.'

'I have thought of it, at least, I have thought about having a small café and a craft shop,' Lys assured her, 'but I've been too busy to do anything more about it. Maybe that's something else you could take in hand?'

Lys was suddenly businesslike, making Dani aware of the drive that had moved her ideas onwards so quickly. 'I've managed to get hold of a cheap computer and printer and got a local printer to put some of Xavier's drawings on to a CD for me. Come on, I'll show you what I've got.'

It didn't take Dani long to get used to the computer set-up and by the following lunchtime, she had designed three different layouts . . . a simple A5 flyer, a folded A4 leaflet and a three-fold one. The final wording had to be discussed and settled upon but the first printings gave a good idea of what the finished products would be like.

Lys was pleased with them and promised to talk over the historical notes with her grandfather over lunch. The huge components of the inner workings of the mill were due to be delivered that afternoon and a sense of excitement was in the air.

Knowing that she would be of little use in the matter, Dani had planned to borrow Lys's bicycle and ride the few kilometres to Le Grand Village where a restored farm had been made into a living museum by a folk group called Les Dejhouqués. She thought it would be beneficial for her to see what other places had to offer so that she could help Lys to plan more ideas for the windmill project.

However, a visit by Alex put that plan on hold.

Christian waved and shouted to her excitedly and demanded to be released from his car seat when he saw the heavy wagon and its contents, but Alex bade him stay where he was. He approached Dani with an apologetic air, picking his way carefully past the stack of components that had already been unloaded.

'I'm sorry to come at such a moment, Dani. I was going to ask if you could mind Christian for a couple of hours but I can see it's bad timing on my part.' He ran his hand distractedly through his hair, feeling that he had been too presumptuous in expecting Dani to come to his rescue without due warning. 'Don't worry about it. I'll think of something else.'

He made as if to move away but Dani laid her hand on his arm.

'Come over here where it's less busy,' she suggested, leading the way nearer to the cottage. Her hand seemed to tingle from the contact with his arm and she was instantly once more aware of the attraction she felt towards him.

She found herself asking, 'What's the problem?'

'I've been called to, er, visit a client, er, quite unexpectedly. Usually Madame Toussaint or Brigitte can come at short notice but, today, neither can make it and Brigitte has only just let me know.'

It was obvious that Alex was far from his usual calm. Recognising this, Dani put aside her misgivings about getting involved with him.

'I'm not part of all this,' waving her hand towards the scene of activity. 'I was going to cycle to Le Grand Village, but I can do that another day. What have you got in mind?'

'Whatever you feel able to offer at such short notice. I'm just relieved you are willing to do it for me. I felt at my wits' end.'

He had looked it, too, but now, with her offer to help, Dani could see his normal poise was returning.

'It's no use having him here,' she reflected aloud, indicating the surroundings with a sweep of her hand. 'As you can see, there's too much going on today for his safety. Shall I take him to the beach?'

'Wonderful! He'll love that. You've saved my sanity.' He grinned delightedly, adding, 'If there weren't so many people around I'd give you a hug.'

Dani felt herself blushing at his spontaneous praise and couldn't help wishing he had hugged her regardless of the people.

'Right!' she said crisply, turning away from him as she spoke. 'Hang on a moment. I'll clear it with Lys and grab a few things to bring with me.'

In less than five minutes, she emerged from the cottage with a bag full of beach things and fully in control of her feelings. This was a neighbourly kindness, nothing more. She had changed into a short, pale blue, strappy sundress and flip-flops and had piled her hair up on top of her head. She put a bottle of water into her bag and a packet of biscuits.

'I'll go by the way of our house in case you need to go home before I return,' Alex said, as he slipped into first gear and eased his car into the road. 'If you're not there when I return, I'll come to the beach to find you. Have you got a mobile phone?'

'Yes . . . fully charged today.'

Dani wrote down her number and tucked the piece of paper into a space on the dashboard. 'Christian isn't allergic to anything, is he?'

Alex grinned sideways at her. 'Not so as you would notice. More to the lack of it, if anything.'

She looked over her shoulder to smile at Christian. 'We'll manage together, won't we, Christian?'

'This is our house coming up on the left,' Alex interrupted, looking in the mirror and slowing down.

He drew up outside a detached, two-storey house in cream-washed stone. The shutters at the windows were dark brown and the window boxes were filled with red, pink and white geraniums. Over the integral garage was a roof-garden with access through wide patio doors from a room on the first floor. The garden was neat and tidy without being in any way notable.

'Madame Toussaint lives next door,' Alex said, nodding towards the house they had just passed. 'She'll be home soon after half-past-six, she said. If you need to go before I return, you could leave Christian with her after that time, but you would have to get Lys to come to collect you, I'm afraid, as Madame Toussaint will be returning on the last bus.' He looked uncomfortable again. 'I'm sorry about all this. Are you sure you don't mind?'

'Of course not. It can't be helped. Don't worry about it. We'll manage fine.'

'Right. I'll take you to the beach, then.'

It wasn't much farther to the beach,

no more than a kilometre or so. Dani was sure Christian would be able to walk back home if necessary. The car park was already full, with cars lining the side of the narrow road leading from Vertbois to the shore.

However, it was designed in a loop with a dropping-off zone nearest to the shore. Alex came to a halt there and helped Dani to unload a bag of beach toys, Christian's towel and her own beach bag then, after kissing Christian goodbye and urging him to be a good boy, he drove off, waving his hand in farewell salutation.

Christian had already tucked his hand trustingly into Dani's, and once he could no longer see his father's car, he looked up at Dani.

'Can we go to the beach now? I want to build a big, big sandcastle.'

'Do you, indeed? Then we had better make a start, hadn't we?'

They trudged expectantly over the saddle-shaped sand-dune, the sound of the Atlantic waves crashing onto the shore growing louder as they neared the top of the rise.

As they crested the top of the dune, a wide expanse of sand confronted them, stretching to the left and right as far as she could see. Although there were over two hundred people scattered over the scene, it seemed by no means crowded.

'Whee! The sea!' Christian shouted, immediately setting off at a run.

'Wait a minute, Christian! Let's set a few rules!' Dani insisted sternly. 'I don't want to lose you!'

'Brigitte lets me run!' he protested.

'Brigitte isn't here.'

She took hold of Christian's hand. 'Look, the sand is dry between us and the sea . . . that means the tide is coming in, so don't start to dig too near it or it will wash away your castle before you've finished it.'

Turning round, she pointed out the small, white hut on top of the dune, near to where they had come over from the car park.

'See that white hut . . . with a flag on

top? That's the life-guard's station. We'll settle in line with it, so if you do happen to wander without me noticing, and I hope you won't, if you find your way back to the hut, our things won't be too far away. Come on, now. We'll find a nice spot just beyond the soft sand . . . that's where the tide came last time, so it's a good place to build our castle. When the tide comes in, it will fill the moat nicely.'

Keeping his shirt and shorts on for the time being, to protect his skin from too much exposure to the sun, Christian eagerly began to dig in the sand. Dani joined him and they worked industriously until a large pile of sand had been made. They patted it, flattened the top, and carefully settled a sand-pie on top.

More sand-pies were deposited around the outer edge of the moat, leaving a space between the two facing the sea, where Dani instructed Christian to start digging a channel that would meet the eventual tide.

'Wow!' Christian admired the structure. 'That's the biggest sandcastle I've ever seen. Can we bring the sea to it now?'

'Not yet. Let's find lots of shells and decorate it. See. Push them into the sand, like this.'

Later, she accompanied Christian down to the sea to collect seawater in his bucket and they tipped the water into the moat. Much to Christian's disappointment, it quickly soaked away and he scurried back to the sea for more. Eventually, Dani persuaded him to wait for the tide and suggested they paddled in the shallow water for a while.

That was great fun. They had taken off their outer clothing and ran, kicking and splashing into the waves. Christian wasn't afraid of the waves knocking him over but Dani hovered nearby to make sure he got to his feet before the next one came.

The afternoon sped by. When the tide approached their castle, Dani moved their belongings out of its way and they cheered with delight when the moat was filled with swirling water. Christian was slightly less excited when the walls of the castle began to crumble but Dani assured him that he would be able to build another castle another day.

She looked at her watch that she had placed in her bag.

'It's nearly five o'clock, Christian. Let's pack up our things and begin to make our way home.'

'Papa said he'd come.' Christian pouted. 'He'll want to see my castle . . . what's left of it.'

'He said he might be back too late. Why don't we get an ice-cream from the vendor and we'll see if I can remember which is your house?'

Making a game of it, Dani encouraged him back along the road. She made him carry his own bucket which he had filled with shells and paused outside some of the houses and chalets they passed, saying, 'Now is it this one,

I wonder? Did it have a well in the garden?'

'No. You're wrong.' Christian chortled, forgetting how far they had come . . . until, suddenly, they were in front of the right house.

There was still no sign of Alex and Dani had made some dinner and played a game or two of Ludo before she heard Alex's car on the drive.

Idiotically, her pulse started to race and she was thankful that she had time to take a few breaths to calm it down whilst he was putting the car into the garage. He came in apologetically, but she assured him it didn't matter. They had had a good time and Christian had been perfectly well behaved.

While he had a quick shower, she made him an omelette with a tossed salad and buttered pieces of the French stick he had brought with him, allowing Christian to switch the television on whilst she was busy.

'I don't deserve this,' Alex smiled, tucking into the omelette, the warmth of his eyes showing the genuineness of his words. ‘You’re spoiling me. I’m not used to it.’

‘You look tired,’ she sympathised. ‘Was it a busy afternoon?’

‘So-so,’ he said, noncommittally. ‘Won’t you join me in a glass of wine, then I won’t feel so guilty about taking your time?’

‘All right.’ She laughed. ‘And then I really must go and I’m sure you’ll want to spend time with Christian before his bedtime.’

‘Look! The clowns, Papa!’ Christian called out, his eyes riveted to the television screen. ‘Are these the naughty clowns or the real ones?’

Alex and Dani both swung their glance to the television. It was evident that the cartoon that Christian had been watching had finished and the early evening news programme was now on. Sure enough, similar clowns to those who had been at the carnival in Le Château a few days ago were cavorting across the screen.

Just as the newscaster was beginning to speak of the breaking news of another daring bank raid that had taken place that afternoon at Jonzac, south of Cognac, Alex picked up the remote control set and switched off the television.

'Papa! I like to see the clowns!' Christian objected. 'Can't I watch them?'

'Not at the moment,' Alex said sharply. 'You know I don't allow you to watch the evening news programme. Besides, we have to take Dani home soon and you haven't told me about your afternoon together yet.'

Dani was taken aback by his sharpness and, although Christian came and sat with them and told his father about the big sandcastle they had made and the way the sea had come and washed it away, she couldn't help but notice an air of distraction in Alex's manner.

Why had he suddenly switched off the television like that? He hadn't minded it being on until the clowns appeared. Whether it was her own misgivings about the incident or Christian's disappointment in not being allowed to see the clowns, Dani couldn't be sure, but the harmony that had been there all afternoon was suddenly gone and Alex didn't object when she repeated her need to return home to see how things had gone on there.

Her misgivings lasted throughout the evening and she couldn't get it out of her mind that there was something in that news item that Alex didn't want his son, or her, to see.

5

The following day, Dani decided to put into operation her plan of involving some of the other artisans at the port in the craft shop at the windmill. Lys, who was busy supervising the work on installing the heavy mechanism that would transfer the power from the sails to the millstone, gave her full sanction.

Dani borrowed Lys's bicycle and rode through the country lanes and cycle routes that eventually led to an idyllic path along the shoreline from the viaduct to the port of the ancient walled town.

She turned her back on the sea and headed away from the port along the road that led to the town. There, she could see that the numerous studio cabins were already open to the public and were enjoying the attention of some of the many tourists who were wandering from cabin to cabin, browsing mostly but sometimes buying.

She made for Xavier's studio first. He had already made numerous charcoal sketches of the windmill in varying sizes and had prepared some canvases prior to painting some in acrylics. She wanted to check that he wouldn't mind if she approached the artist who did watercolours, not wanting to put any discord between him and Lys.

He was busy sketching a young mother with a squirming toddler on her lap but he gave her a brief nod of acknowledgement as she approached him. A glance over his shoulder showed her the depth of his talent and she slowly walked around the cabin, looking at the pictures of local scenes and a variety of wildlife displayed on its walls.

Some were in charcoal, others in pastels, all sprayed with a fixative to prevent them being smudged by careless handling.

When at last she was able to share

her objective with him, Xavier made no objection to the proposal.

'The more variety, the better,' he agreed. 'Now, why don't you sit down and I'll sketch your portrait whilst you are here? Have you time?'

'At the speed that you do your sketches, yes!' She laughed, sitting on the stool recently vacated by the previous satisfied client. 'Don't you get fed up of drawing portraits all day long?'

'I don't do it all day long. When I have had enough, I either do some other work whilst people browse around my studio, or I close shop and travel around the island looking for more inspiration.'

His glance flickered from Dani's face to his easel as he spoke, the thin stick of charcoal in his fingers seeming to dart here and there across the sheet of paper. He smiled his attractive, lazy smile that Dani knew had melted Lys' heart.

A momentary flicker of memory of

Alex's face disturbed her mind but it was gone before she had time to dwell on its relevance. There were too many complications there, the most recent being his sudden closing in of himself after his switching off of the news item last night. She wasn't even sure she wanted to dig beneath the surface, in spite of the feral attraction that his presence aroused within her.

'Voila!' Xavier announced with a flourish, spraying the fixative over his sketch and whipping it off his easel. 'Here you are, mademoiselle!'

Dani took the sketch and studied it critically. He had captured the essence of her character, neither flattering nor fault-finding but showing her as she was.

'I like it,' she nodded, standing up and fiddling with the clasp of her shoulder bag to get out her purse.

Xavier waved his hand, dismissing her gesture. 'It is my pleasure, Dani. You are a friend. Please accept it as my gift to you.'

'That's kind of you. Thank you. May I leave it here until Lys comes in her car later? She said I was to ask you to come for supper. She wants to work late, to get as much as possible of the renovated machinery installed in the windmill before the weekend. We've already had a few tentative enquiries about when it will be open to the public.'

Xavier agreed and, gratified by his friendship, she then sauntered around the other studios, speaking to each of the artists and craftsmen and women of what they could offer. The maker of silver jewellery wanted only to offer items already made, but the potter, the watercolour artist and the artisan who fashioned all manner of things in glass were willing to create items specifically related to the windmill.

Marcel, the potter, was especially enthusiastic, suggesting a number of ideas, from model windmills of varying sizes, with sails that would revolve at a touch of the finger or a puff of wind, to

3D wall-mounts and bowls. In fact, he was still pouring out suggestions when he realised that the other artisans were closing their exhibitions for a lunchtime break, and he invited Dani to accompany him to a local café.

It was while waiting for the order to be served that Dani caught sight of the headline in a newspaper being read by another customer at the next table. It read, *Copy-cat raid of Oléron bank-snatch kills clown impersonator.*

Dani caught her breath. That was what Alex hadn't wanted his son to see! One of the bank-raiders, dressed as a clown had been shot by the police after a tip-off. But, how had Alex known about it? Known that it would be included in the news item? The information had only just been released, the newscaster had said.

Had Alex been present? A customer in the bank when it happened? Was that the town where his business meeting had taken place? But why hadn't he made some mention of it? Had he been afraid it would lead to more questions from Christian?

It was none of her business, she reflected, nonetheless relieved to have an acceptable reason for his sharpness. Having sole charge of a young child couldn't be easy. He must miss his wife very much.

'So is that all right by you?' she suddenly heard Marcel ask.

'Pardon? Sorry! I was miles away! What was it you said?'

'I asked if I might visit the windmill, to get a good idea of its style and character,' Marcel patiently repeated.

'Yes, of course. In fact, why not come with Xavier to supper tonight? I'm trying out a new recipe I found on a postcard, Moules à Basquaise. Do you like mussels?'

'I like anything to do with food,' he replied with a grin. 'I'll bring a bottle of wine, shall I?'

'Great! Lys will come for you both about eight o'clock. That should give you enough time to look over the place and sketch some dimensions.'

Pleased with her morning's work, Dani cycled back to Le Deu via Le Grand Village, where she made the self-guided tour of the reconstructed mediaeval farmstead with the help of a printed leaflet.

Dani called at the patisserie to buy some long French sticks and some ciabatta bread that Madame Giraud had earlier promised to save under the counter.

'You're sure you don't want to join us?' Dani asked, having taken an instant liking to the homely woman.

'We wouldn't dream of it, Dani! Etienne and I will do very nicely here, thank you. We're not so old that we've forgotten what it's like to be young!'

Dani laughed and said she was sure they hadn't. She thought the couple got on remarkably well together, though Lys denied that there was any middle-aged romance going on under their noses. Dani wasn't so convinced, though she didn't argue the point with her friend.

Etienne was there at the windmill when she returned home. His animated face showed his joy at seeing the windmill come to life in front of him. He had already taken apart, polished and re-assembled the small working-model he had made years ago for Lys . . . and had explained in minute detail to Dani how the system worked. She felt as excited as he did as she now saw it all coming together, sharing the disappointment that it couldn't be completed today.

'The light will go before it could be finished,' Lys commiserated with them. 'They're coming back tomorrow at eight o'clock in the morning, so no lying in bed tomorrow for any of us!'

* * *

Once the workmen had stopped for the day and Etienne had ambled back to his temporary lodgings, Lys drove to Le Château to pick up Xavier and Marcel, leaving Dani to scrub the mussels and remove their beards, chop an onion and a clove of garlic, peel and chop some tomatoes, and grate some breadcrumbs, ready to be cooked in half a litre of white wine, when Xavier and Marcel had spent as much time as they needed looking at the windmill whilst there was still enough light left to do so.

As it happened, Lys was so excited about relating every aspect of the renovations to them all, she insisted that Dani included herself in the impromptu conducted tour and, along with Xavier and Marcel, Dani obediently followed her throughout the three floors of the windmill and listened intently to all the information lovingly imparted.

It was interesting and Dani stored a great many details in her mind to be brought out later when she was editing and finalising the drafts of the various leaflets in her charge.

Marcel, seeing and hearing it for the first time, had many spontaneous questions to ask which elicited yet more information and Dani recognised in his face the enthusiasm of creativity that was buzzing about in his head.

Lys was delighted with Marcel's response, and included Dani and Xavier in her expressed appreciation. The four of them were standing in a close group, arms loosely along each other's shoulders as they gazed back at the windmill, each with his or her own thoughts of its imminent new birth.

'It really is going to be a success, isn't it!' Lys stated rather than asked, her face glowing as she sought assurance from her three companions.

'Certainement!'

'Bien sûr!'

'Of course!'

The three spoke in unison, just as Dani sensed, rather than saw or heard, a car pulling up behind them. She twisted her head round and instantly recognised it as Alex's car. She lifted her hand from Marcel's shoulder to wave a welcome, frowning slightly as Alex's face lost its glow.

Alex instantly reproved himself for the slight twinge of pique he felt at seeing Dani's arms entwined around the shoulders of a man much nearer in age to Dani than he himself was. The girl was entitled to have a boyfriend, wasn't she?

And why had he felt the need to explain his brusqueness of the previous evening? Dani probably hadn't even noticed how swiftly he had reacted to the news item. Why should she? It was just one of many disturbing daily events of modern life.

Maybe he should have been more open with her from the start? On the other hand . . . ? His eyes narrowed as he took in the two young men, his gaze lingering on Xavier, then back to the other man. Was Xavier Monsigny's presence on the island as innocent as Dani and Lys believed? Or was there a more sinister reason?

He raised his right hand in a casual wave and switched off the engine. It was as good a time as any to be introduced to Xavier Monsigny and his fellow artist . . . for that was what he seemed. Who knows, a few discreet questions might save time and man-power later.

'Hello, there!' he greeted the quartet, his smile encompassing them all. 'Hi, Dani! I was just passing by and wondered how far along the windmill project is coming. There's a lot less stuff out here, so I conclude it's been installed in place?'

'All but the sails,' Lys agreed, performing the necessary introductions between the men, waiting before saying more as they shook hands.

'Are you local?' Alex asked Marcel casually.

'No, a summer visitor, bringing my skills with me, like the rest of our crowd.'

'Your crowd?'

'The artisans at the port. And yourself?'

'From Dijon originally, but lately from Paris,' Alex replied, adding before asked, 'I'm here with my young son, trying to mix work with holidays before he starts school.'

'Not easy!' Lys sympathised, knowing of his child-minding problems from Dani.

'No,' he agreed lightly. 'I'm getting to be a good 'juggler' of time and resources.'

He turned his attention to the two men. 'Did you all know each other before you came here? Dani tells me you're a friendly bunch,' he added, hoping he didn't sound too patronising.

He smiled at Dani and then studied the exterior aspect of the windmill, making his question sound more like a casual remark more than a serious enquiry.

'Free spirits, the lot of us,' Marcel commented casually. 'No roots, no chains.'

His eyes seemed to seek Dani's and Alex wondered if he were trying to tell her something. He probably fancied her like mad. Was the feeling shared, he wondered, recognising in himself a lingering resurgence of adolescent jealousy.

Dani, however, disentangled herself from the group, announcing lightly, 'I'm going to start to cook supper.'

'Want any help?' Marcel asked.

'No, thanks. It's all prepared. What about you, Alex? Can you stay? There's enough to go round. I bought plenty.'

He appreciated her inclusion of him but wasn't sure he wanted to spend the evening warring with Marcel for her favours. She probably thought him too old for her, anyway, which he was, if he were entirely honest and less self-centred. And hadn't he already decided, like Marcel, no entanglements?

Even so, his smile held genuine regret for his refusal. 'Thanks for the invitation. I appreciate it, but I must get back home. Madame Toussaint will be getting anxious, and, as you know, Christian likes me home before he goes to bed. May I bring him to see the windmill when it is up and running? He is pestering me continually about it.'

'Of course! In fact we're going to have an opening ceremony,' Lys interrupted. 'You must come to that, and your kind neighbour. The more, the merrier!'

Dani watched from the kitchen window as Alex departed, a curious mixture of emotions in her heart. Wasn't that what she wanted? Hadn't Marcel put it succinctly, no roots, no chains? She wasn't ready for the chains of instant motherhood, was she?

So why did her heart feel so desolate as the car disappeared from sight?

6

It took three days to assemble the four sails and attach them securely to the main shaft that turned the first cog. The huge wooden rudder was then fitted to the opposite side of the conical roof, so that the roof could be painstakingly manhandled around the three hundred and sixty degrees of the compass until the sails were in the best position to catch the wind.

'And this might have to be done any number of times a day, depending on the fickleness of the wind!' Etienne commented.

His words might have been taken as a grumble, until the expression of pride on his face or in his voice was noticed! Dani had never seen him so animated.

'At least I now know why there are two doors into the windmill!' she declared with a laugh.

'It's far better than having to dodge the sails on your way in or out!' Lys agreed. 'You'll notice we always keep one door locked!'

They had all prayed for sufficient wind to be blowing. No-one wanted this first testing of the sails to be powered by electricity, and they weren't disappointed. The linen sails were already full and straining to go and, accompanied by a loud cheer that must have been heard all over the island, the sails began to turn.

Dani was surprised to see tears streaming down Etienne's face but, when she touched her own cheeks, they too were wet with tears. There was barely a dry eye between them as they all hugged each other or held hands and danced in circles.

Although it wasn't the official opening ceremony, a number of people had gathered, Alex and Christian among them, and Dani found herself being swept off her feet and swung around by a grinning Alex, with Christian hanging on to her shorts and jumping up and down in excitement.

It seemed quite natural when Alex set her down on to her feet that he gathered her into his arms and kissed her soundly on her lips, and it took a few seconds before either of them realised what he had done, and they sprang apart.

'I'm sorry!' Alex apologised immediately, looking appallingly contrite! 'I got carried away by the excitement.'

Before Dani could respond, he turned to Christian and swept him up into the air. 'It was very exciting, wasn't it, son?'

'Yes! Yes! Round and round they go! Whee!'

Dani was glad Alex's attention had left her because she hadn't been sorry at all that he had kissed her. Surprised, yes. Sorry? No. Her fingers tentatively touched her tingling lips, wondering if they looked as different as they felt.

She had been startled, and had only just begun to respond when Alex had leaped away from her. Had it been so distasteful to him that he couldn't bear to prolong the kiss a second longer? He looked as if he already regretted his impulsive action.

Dani hastily glanced around. Had anyone noticed the short encounter? But no-one seemed to have done so, or, if they had, thought nothing of it. Lys and Xavier seemed as bright-eyed as she felt, but their kiss had been one of many, not a first, like hers had been — and likely to be the last, she reflected ruefully, watching Alex still cavorting with his son.

Chagrined to think how little the kiss had meant to Alex, Dani swung abruptly round and stalked over to the group of workmen, determined to act as if nothing of importance had taken place.

She missed Alex's rueful expression as he watched her stalk away. He fingered his chin between this thumb and first finger for a moment or so, his thoughts unreadable

'What's the matter, Papa?' Christian asked, puzzled by his father's silent contemplation.

Pulled back to reality, Alex smiled down at him. 'Nothing, son, except I think I just upset Dani.'

'You could kiss her better, like you do to me,' Christian suggested helpfully.

Alex laughed humourlessly. 'That might make it worse,' he commented wryly. 'It might be best if we just slip away.'

And when Dani next looked round for them, they had gone.

Nobody else seemed to notice and Dani followed Etienne into the windmill. The romantic, lazy image of the windmill's exterior was shattered immediately. The heavy pounding of the motion of the sails was almost unbearable and she felt like putting her hands over her ears to block out the sound. How on earth did the miller cope with its assault upon his ears and other senses all day long?

The brake was eventually re-applied

and everything re-checked to make sure nothing had worked loose with the rhythmic motion. When all was declared satisfactory, Etienne decided to put the first lot of grain through.

'Just to test the system,' he declared, as if anyone might suspect him of wanting to see the windmill in action for any other reason.

They had bought a wagonload of sacks of grain, all of highest quality. 'We'll do all our baking from it,' Lys had insisted.

Madame Giraud had agreed. 'I might not bake as much as I used to,' she apologised, 'but I'll only buy your flour from now on.'

'I think you might be baking more than you realise, Madame Giraud,' Dani reminded her. 'Once we're up and running, we're expecting people to buy snacks from us. We'll have to go carefully to start with, estimate the demand, and all that, but I think that, eventually, we'll be able to sell all that you can make.'

'There'll be none more pleased than I, if that's the case,' Madame Giraud replied, looking pleased. 'People will soon remember how much better homemade bread and pastries taste.'

The official opening had been set for the Wednesday of the following week, a few days before the annual French August holidays began. Their painted signboards would be finished by then and displayed in appropriate places. Reception, Ticket Office, Car Park, Refreshments and Souvenirs . . . and the two largest, proclaiming Le Moulin de Deu on the outer wall of the mill itself and over the car park entrance.

Dani ran off a large number of posters that they were going to place in local tourist offices, supermarkets and wherever anyone would give them permission to post them.

The heading of Dani's bright poster proclaimed it to be, *The official opening to the only working windmill on Ile d'Oléron*.

'With that in mind, Dani,' Lys

hesitantly began to say, 'Would you mind if I left you in charge here tomorrow? I've been in contact with the proprietors of the nearest working windmill on the mainland at Marans, a few kilometres north of La Rochelle.'

'Yes, that's fine by me,' Dani agreed. 'There's nothing much happening here, anyway. If we get any visitors, I think I can manage to show them round now, and no doubt your grandfather will run the sails.'

* * *

A trickle of visitors presented themselves throughout the day and Dani reckoned it to be an easy way in to what they could expect it to be like once the main holiday month was under way.

The only blot to the day was when Alex called with his usual request for Dani to look after Christian for a few hours. She hadn't seen him since the day the sails first went round and she regretted having to refuse Alex's request.

As usual, also, the necessity was immediate and Alex had no time to spare to do anything other than look crestfallen and then be over-apologetic for assuming her to be free.

'Never mind. I'll have to think of something else,' he said over his shoulder as he turned back to his car.

'I'm really sorry.' Dani called after him, not wanting to think she was simply being unhelpful. 'Any other time.'

But she wasn't sure he had heard her.

Her inability to help and Alex's swift departure niggled at her throughout the afternoon and as soon as Etienne decided it was time to close for the day, Dani quickly gathered together their day's takings, made sure the bookwork was complete and left a note for Lys to say where she was going.

She then hauled out Lys's bike and set off without delay towards Vertbois. It was already after seven o'clock and she fully expected Alex to be back or that Madame Toussaint would be seeing to Christian's bath-time . . . but it was Brigitte who came to the door in answer to her knock.

'Oh, it's you,' Brigitte said ungraciously. 'Monsieur Gallepe said you wouldn't look after Christian for him, so he asked me instead. I said I would always try to oblige him, as long as he pays double after six o'clock.'

Brigitte had the telephone clamped between her ear and her shoulder as she spoke and the slender emery board that she held poised in her left hand showed that she was also in the process of filing her nails.

'I just came to see if Alex, Monsieur Gallepe, had managed to make satisfactory arrangements,' Dani haltingly explained. 'Since you're here, I may as well go.'

The sound of the television blaring away in the living room gave an indication of where Christian was, even though Dani knew he was usually getting ready for bed by now. Still, it wasn't for her to interfere in Alex's domestic arrangements.

She half-turned to leave but was drawn back when Brigitte spoke again, not to her, Dani belatedly realised, but to whoever was on the other end of the telephone conversation.

'Yes, it's that woman I told you about, the one who got me into trouble the other day at the park,' Brigitte spoke into the telephone. 'What? Oh! Yes, why not. The kid never does as he's told, anyway. I'll tell her.' She stepped aside slightly, saying, 'You'd better come in. My boyfriend says that since you're here now, we may as well go out as planned, I'll see you at the end of the lane in five minutes,' the latter being addressed to the telephone. She made kissing noises with her lips and stabbed at the 'off' button with a long-taloned finger.

'That was my boyfriend,' she added unnecessarily to Dani, thrusting the phone into her hand. It obviously wasn't her own mobile she had been using. 'I'm off, then. Don't forget to tell

Monsieur Gallepe he owes me until eight o'clock — I don't do part-hours. I'll call for my money, that is unless you'd like to pay me now? No? Please yourself. He'd pay you back, he never quibbles. He's quite a softie, really!'

And with that carefree approbation of Alex's character, Brigitte waltzed over the threshold, down the path and through the gate without a backward glance, whilst Dani was still drawing in her breath and gathering her wits together.

She was wondering what Alex would say on his return to find himself with a different childminder, when Christian burst into the hallway and skidded to a standstill.

'Dani! I thought I heard your voice! Have you come to play with me? Where's Brigitte gone?'

At least one member of the Gallepe household was pleased to see her, Dani reflected.

'She had to go out,' she said to Christian. 'Now, isn't it your bath-time and bed-time, young man?'

Christian giggled. 'I'm not really a 'young man', am I?'

'That depends on how long it takes us to put your toys away and get your bath ready. Double-quick and you might get a story as well.'

'And can I watch a video? Brigitte said I could.'

'We'll save that for another day, shall we?'

A rebellious look was about to take root on his face but Dani ignored it and swooped forward, growling like a teddy bear. 'I'm coming to get you!'

With a squeal, Christian ran back into the living room and a noisy ten minutes saw all the toys put away and the bathwater running into the bath — twenty minutes play in soap bubbles came to an end when she pulled the plug out and when Christian was wrapped in a large fluffy towel, Dani set to search for his pyjamas.

'They'll be in the cupboard on the landing,' Christian told her. 'That one, over there. No, not that one. The next.'

Dani had already pulled open the first cupboard door and was about to shut it again when her eyes settled upon something extraordinary hanging in the cupboard. Disbelievingly, she reached into the cupboard and unhooked the hanger . . . and pulled out an adult-sized clown costume, exactly the same as the ones worn by the clowns at the carnival and the robbers in the bank raid! A curly orange wig dangled from the hook at the top.

Now, what would Alex Gallepe be doing with a clown outfit in his house?

Behind her, Christian giggled. 'Papa is sometimes a clown!' He grinned. 'He was in the carnival the day you found me.'

'Was he indeed?'

She remembered Christian saying, 'I can see Papa,' during the bank raid. Her eyes narrowed thoughtfully.

'And did you see him at any other time?'

Christian frowned. 'I'm not sure. I

thought I did, but Papa said he didn't fire a gun. Only bad men fire guns, don't they? Papa isn't a bad man.'

'Of course he's not,' Dani instinctively agreed quickly, but the sight of the clown outfit gave her doubts.

'We'll put this away and keep Papa's secret, shall we?' she said, more lightheartedly than she felt. Was it an innocent clown outfit, even with its distinctive orange wig? Lots of people dress up as clowns for children's parties and such, didn't they? Not all that many, her reason contradicted.

Christian wrinkled his face. 'I do like clowns, at least, I did, until the bad clowns fired guns. Not all clowns have guns, do they?'

'No, of course not.'

She tousled his hair fondly. 'I think I saw one of your story books was about a clown, 'The Youngest Clown In The Circus', isn't it? Let's get you into your pyjamas and I'll read it to you whilst your drink your milk.'

The diversion seemed to take

Christian's mind off his worries about bad clowns and after listening to the story twice, he willingly settled down to sleep. Dani wished she could settle as easily. She didn't want to make a fool of herself by asking Alex outright about the clown outfit, neither did she want to put him into a position of having to lie about it to her, though why she should be quite so sensitive about his feelings, she didn't know. And how was she going to react to him face-to-face when he returned?

She was spared that necessity, at least.

A knock on the door heralded a visit from Madame Toussaint, who was clearly expecting to see Brigitte open the door. In face of her confusion, Dani hurriedly explained who she was and the reason for her being there in Brigitte's place.

'She is a thoroughly unreliable girl!' Madame Toussaint commented with tight lips. 'I don't know why Monsieur Gallepe continues to employ her.'

'Maybe he has no choice?' Dani suggested mildly.

'What that man needs is a wife, and a mother for his son,' Madame Toussaint declared, her eyes seeming to be weighing up Dani as a possible applicant.

Dani could only smile and remain silent. The post had its attractions but she wasn't sure that they outweighed the disadvantages.

Remembering the purpose of her call, Madame Toussaint drew her thoughts together.

'Monsieur Gallepe has telephoned to say he will be very late and he has asked me to take over here. Of course, he thought Brigitte would be here, not you, so if you think he would prefer you to stay, mademoiselle . . . ?'

She left the rest of her sentence hanging in the air but Dani saw it as a way out of facing Alex with the discovery of the clown's outfit still fresh in her mind and decided to take advantage of it. Besides, it was still light enough to ride her bike along the country lanes, and she was sure that someone of Madame Toussaint's generation would think it unseemly for an unmarried young lady to sleep in the house of an attractive unattached man!

'Thank you, madame. It's very kind of you. Christian is fast asleep, so there is no problem of him being upset by the change.'

And Dani cycled back to the windmill with her thoughts in turmoil. What exactly was she getting mixed up with? And, fond as she was becoming of Christian, would she be foolish to continue to be associated with his father?

7

On her return to the windmill cottage, Dani discovered that Lys had already been home, read her note and taken herself off to Le Château to meet Xavier.

Dani was relieved to realise that she had the rest of the evening to herself. It would give her time to sort out her fluctuating thoughts before having to try to act as if nothing untoward had happened, and she and Lys were such close friends that it could be difficult to maintain any deception.

She checked over the layout and wording of the leaflets she had designed and ran off one of each for Lys to verify the following day, and then she took herself off to her bedroom. It was only half-past ten but she still felt weighed down by the events of the latter part of the day.

She felt it a bit cowardly of her not wanting to risk still being up when Lys came home, but was honest enough to admit to herself that she had to sort things out in her own mind first, before she would be ready to talk about what had happened with anybody else, even someone as close to her as Lys.

She spent much of the long night going over her involvement with Alex and Christian. On one front, her involvement was slight, even though their first meeting had been unconventional and fairly traumatic. Was that why it had made such an impact on her life?

Since then, their meetings had been of a casual nature and, apart from once having lunch with Alex, they had been brief and almost businesslike, apart from that one kiss. Her lips curved into a faint smile as she relived the memory and she once more traced the kiss with the tips of her fingers.

It had been no more than an irrational, spontaneous reaction to the excitement of the occasion, she told herself sharply. It meant nothing whatsoever to Alex.

It had meant everything to her. It had brought her true feelings for Alex into the open, for her, at least. She had enjoyed his kiss. She had wanted it to go on and on, and she wanted it to happen again.

Something leaped between them every time they met. The question was, was it the same for Alex? She couldn't be sure, and his reaction after kissing her wasn't exactly the reaction of a man smitten by love.

She sighed. She would have to accept that she was experiencing a one-way love affair.

But people don't really fall in love so quickly, she reasoned. At least, not ordinary people like herself.

And then, there was all this nonsense about clowns. Why shouldn't Alex have a clown outfit to amuse his son? It didn't need to have a more sinister meaning, did it?

And yet, it did. It lurked in the back of her mind all the time. What was she to do? If she challenged Alex, and if he were guilty, she would either have to end all association with him there and then — or, agree to accept his guilt and get into a deeper relationship with him, and become an accomplice after the fact.

If he were innocent, and surely he was, he would despise her suspicions of him and wouldn't want to have anything more to do with her. Could she face that?

She decided she couldn't.

She seemed to lie awake for ages and, when sleep finally settled upon her, she slept restlessly. When she awoke the following day she felt worse than if she'd had a night on the tiles.

Lys greeted her enthusiastically. She had had a successful day at the other windmill and felt confident that they were on the right lines here at Le Deu.

'The visitors wanted to know about the history of the windmill, as well as how it worked,' she explained, too thrilled by the success of her visit to notice Dani's uncharacteristic quietness. 'Someone in each group seemed to ask the right questions and Rodrigue, the main guide, could explain and describe everything.'

Lys looked over Dani's printed leaflets and gave her the go-ahead to run them off on the printer they had installed in the rear portion of what was beginning to take shape as the craft shop.

The printer was churning out the third batch when Alex's car pulled into the car park.

'You've got a visitor, Dani,' Lys called out with a grin.

Dani's heart skipped a beat. This was 'make-your-mind-up' time. She could either tell him that she didn't think it was such a good idea for them to pursue their relationship any further, and risk him saying, 'What relationship?' Or she could pretend nothing had happened and agree to whatever he had come to ask.

Her face must have betrayed some of her feelings because, when she stepped outside to meet him, Alex strode towards her, his hands outstretched, saying, 'Dani! My most humble apologies! Whatever must you think of me and the haphazard arrangements I seem to be forever making for Christian's care? Forgive me once again for involving you in such a way.'

Dani swallowed hard, her night-long turmoil still unresolved. 'That's all right,' she said weakly, wondering how her hands had come to be held in Alex's firm grasp. 'I felt bad about not being able to help you when you came earlier yesterday afternoon, and I just wanted to make sure you had managed to arrange something.'

'And found that little minx, Brigitte, holding the fort. She was the best I could do at such short notice.'

His easy grin took some severity out of his words and Dani knew it was only small-talk. Feeling completely unnerved by his closeness, her various strategies having flown right out of her mind, she merely gabbled, 'You pay her too much. She takes advantage of your generosity.'

Alex gently squeezed her hands, his eyes dark and serious. 'Nothing is too much where Christian is concerned, but I agree that Brigitte takes advantage. I wish I didn't need to engage her services. Christian doesn't really take to her, like he has to you. He has become quite attached to you. I don't suppose . . . ?'

He left his sentence unfinished, although Dani wasn't really aware of that. All she knew was that all of her body was trembling. What was the matter with her?

His eyes held hers and she wondered why she hadn't realised before just how dark they were. They seemed to be as dark as the midnight sky and her mind was whisked back to the day of the carnival, and her impromptu whirling jig with the orange-haired clown with his dark laughing eyes.

'It was you, wasn't it?' she burst out without thinking, her face flushing with the realisation. Christian had said his dad was there. Why hadn't it occurred to her before? Ashamedly, she knew the reason — she had been too ready to look for a sinister reason for the clown suit belonging to Alex. How could she?

Alex was smiling sheepishly at her, looking a little discomfited. 'What was me?' he asked, without regard to grammar, his voice betraying that he knew the answer.

Dani's mind felt relieved from all her suspicions. There was no bad motive for the clown outfit hanging in the cupboard at his home. He had been part of the carnival procession, that was all!

'The clown at the carnival! You danced with me. Why didn't you say? You must have recognised me when we met later.'

Alex's beguiling awkwardness increased, melting her reserves yet further. He shrugged his shoulders helplessly.

'When I met you with Christian, it

was hardly the best of times to acknowledge our earlier encounter. I was breathing fire, remember. And, afterwards, the moment seemed to have passed. I didn't want to place you under any sense of obligation to me.' He smiled wryly. 'Nor did I want to discover that our caper had had no meaning to you.' He hesitated, then added softly, 'It did to me, you see.'

His eyes once again seemed to glow with an indefinable light and Dani felt a swirl of melting fire spiral through her.

'It, it did to me, as well,' she confessed hesitantly. 'When you let go of my hands and danced away, it felt as though I had lost someone special.'

'I kept wondering if you would recognise me again, and was disappointed when you didn't. It made me think I had imagined it, or that it had only affected me.'

'Something was there, though,' Dani said in wonder. 'But I didn't recognise it as being the same. I've been fighting it, really.'

'And now?'

Dani felt some of the elation drain from her. There were still reservations to consider. Christian, for one thing. Alex had already said how attached to her Christian was becoming. What if things didn't work out between her and Alex? It would be a double blow to the child.

'I'm not sure,' she said flatly. 'There's Christian . . . '

She feared that Alex might misunderstand her meaning, perhaps thinking that she didn't feel she could take to the child, but he didn't. His face sobered.

'Yes. He's desperate to have a new mama. It's not that he's forgotten Trudi, really. Although I'm sure his memory of her is fading. He misses the intensity of the love she gave him. A father's love is different and I sometimes find it hard to be both father and mother to him. However,' he added pointedly, 'I am not on the lookout for a new mother for Christian, but, rather, a new wife for myself.'

He looked intently into her eyes. 'She will have to be a very special person,' he said softly. 'She will have to fulfil both parts, you see.'

Her heart lurched. 'And you're not sure that I can do that?'

'I think you probably can, but that puts you under an impossible strain. No room for error. No room for second thoughts.'

Dani nodded. His reservations matched her own so neatly. She thought she knew, but what if she were wrong?

'So, what do we do?' she asked quietly, her heart filling with hopelessness. Were they to lose their chance of happiness for fear of making a mistake? 'Do we stop before we begin? Is that what you're saying?'

A sort of pain gripped her heart. Not a physical pain, nothing like that. It was an emotional pain, a pain of fear of loss and she felt the strength flowing out of her body.

Somehow, Alex was aware of the pain that gripped her, it matched the anguish in his own heart. Impulsively, he enveloped her in his arms. 'No, no, my love!'

He caressed her cheeks with his fingertips, drawing a line along her cheekbones until he reached her trembling mouth, and traced around her lips, almost overcome by the depth of his feelings for her.

He hadn't meant to kiss her out here in the middle of the deserted car park but he was unable to stop himself. His lips found hers and they kissed with an intensity that rocked his senses.

It had to end. They breathlessly drew apart, laughing with joy at the delight they had experienced.

'Loving brings risks,' he mused, ' . . . but I'm willing to take them. How about you?'

Dani nodded, her eyes sombre. 'Yes. I've been trying to deny that I was falling in love with you. Fighting it, even, but I can't fight it any longer, not after a kiss like that.'

She shook her head, as if recognising

the foolishness of fighting such a force. 'But we must go carefully,' she insisted, still having reservations about being able to be a capable mother to a vulnerable four-year child. 'We mustn't risk building up Christian's hopes and hurting him.'

'Agreed! I don't want to risk hurting you, either,' he said, smiling tenderly at her. 'I've been married before but you haven't, and I respect that. I'll not compromise you in any way, but I do have a proposition to put to you.'

His eyes searched her for permission to proceed and continued, 'I can't let things go on in the haphazard way I have been doing. Just for the next few weeks, I need a 'live-in' carer for Christian. Brigitte's no use. Madame Toussaint has been wonderful, almost like the grand-mother he hasn't got. But she has other responsibilities and is too elderly to be a full-time carer.'

He hardly dared to continue. He knew he would be asking a lot of Dani but he hoped she wouldn't refuse him out of hand.

'This has nothing to do with us discovering how we feel about each other,' he began firmly. 'It was the real purpose of my visit, until we got sidetracked.'

Again he hesitated but knew he had to go on. 'The thing is, Dani, will you consider being Christian's full-time carer?'

8

His question seemed to hang in the air between them. Dani's face betrayed her complete amazement and Alex knew he had to follow up his opening gambit with a few details.

'I would want you to live in, if you agree to my proposition, but I assure you that it will be totally a business deal.' He smiled faintly. 'I've been without a wife for a year. I can manage to control my emotions for a while longer. I'm saying this to assure you that my intentions are completely honourable.'

He held his breath as Dani considered what he had asked of her.

Slowly, she nodded. 'I'll have to clear it with Lys, of course. She was willing to give me a job when I didn't have one and I don't want to let her down.'

When it was put to her, Lys wasn't

totally surprised by Dani's request. She had seen the intense embrace. 'Go for it, kid! He seems nice and Christian obviously likes you, and you've got a retreat to come running back to if things don't work out. Go with my blessing.'

Dani felt a bit sad as Alex drove her away. It was one part of her life, albeit a short part, closing down, but she was also excited about moving in with Alex and Christian.

'Does Christian know I'm coming?' she asked Alex.

'No. I didn't dare raise his hopes.' He glanced sideways at her. 'No regrets?'

'No. As you said, it will give us a chance to see how things work out.'

Christian was busy doing a jigsaw, watched over by Madame Toussaint. He looked up and smiled with delight when he saw Dani.

'Hello! Have you come to play with me? Are you going out, Papa?'

Dani answered, 'Yes.'

And Alex answered, 'No.'

They laughed and Alex added, 'Dani is going to be your childminder from now on. What do you say to that?'

'Forever?' Christian asked.

'Well, for the rest of the summer,' Dani replied.

'And what then?'

'By then, you'll be ready for school and we'll see how things go.'

'Do I have to be very good, so that you'll stay?'

Dani laughed. 'I don't expect you to suddenly become angelic! It's me who's on trial, not you.'

Dani could hear Alex explaining their business arrangement to Madame Toussaint which, she admitted, she was old-fashioned enough to appreciate.

Madame Toussaint seemed to find nothing amiss with it. 'I will still be available to sit with Christian when Mademoiselle Cachart has time off,' she volunteered, making Dani realise that she had agreed to the deal without any mention of either hours of duty or rate of pay. A fine businesswoman she was.

When Madame Toussaint had left them, Alex showed her to her room. It was set out as a bed-sit.

'Of course, you must feel free to use the rest of the house, whether I am home or not,' Alex hastened to explain. 'You are to treat the house as your home. I specially took this house because of this arrangement. It will give you a place of privacy that is solely for your own use. I don't expect you to become my cook and housekeeper. I have a cleaner who comes in three times a week and I usually cook my own dinner, or buy a take-away.'

'You never know,' he added with a grin, 'we might even get the chance of the occasional meal out, with the help of Madame Toussaint! However, it will be a help if you agree to prepare and supervise Christian's meals, of course. Now, is there anything I've forgotten?'

'I suppose I ought to enquire about my hours and rate of pay,' she suggested mildly.

'Of course! How remiss of me. Shall we say any evening I am in, you can count as your own, though I hope you will stay in for some of them?' He raised an eyebrow enquiringly at her and Dani blushed.

'Yes, of course.' Her heart raced at the thought.

'And you must have at least one day a week free, plus Sunday. Can you be flexible on that? My hours of work are sometimes a bit unpredictable, as, no doubt, you've noticed. As for rate of pay?' He mentioned a sum that made Dani's eyes widen.

'That's far too much!' she protested.

Alex shook his head. 'When I said that Christian is worth any amount, I meant it. Now, come here! A quick kiss before Christian comes to see what we're doing!'

Dani gladly stepped forward into his open arms and melted into his embrace. He kissed her tenderly at first, savouring the sweetness of her, but, as their passion arose, the kiss deepened. Dani felt that she couldn't get enough of him and hungered greedily for more.

When she heard a small moan deep within them, she was startled to realise that it came from her and when they reluctantly pulled apart, she was surprised to find that her feet were still on the ground. She had felt almost disembodied, floating somewhere above them.

They spent the rest of the morning on the beach, digging in the sand, playing with a ball and splashing in and out of the sea, for all the world as if they were a real family. Dani found it satisfying and began to feel herself being less anxious about taking on another woman's child.

This was the easy part, she acknowledged. It wouldn't always be as idyllic as this. Life never was.

* * *

They had a late lunch back at the house and then Alex left to attend a meeting somewhere on the mainland, he said. 'But I'll be back early evening so that you can help Lys distribute those advertising leaflets.'

He was as good as his word and Dani cycled back to the windmill, arriving just before a group of the artisans from the port set out with a handful of leaflets each. Lys paired them off and told them which area to cover.

Dani found herself with Marcel, who seemed a little put-out by her change of status.

'You're throwing yourself away as a children's nanny?' he scorned. 'I thought you'd have more discrimination than that.'

'It's to help a friend,' she explained. 'Just like we're now helping Lys, and she is helping all of you by promoting your work. Xavier has already sold more pictures by having them on display here, and we're not even open properly yet.'

'Not that he needs much help!' Marcel retorted in aggrieved tones.

'What do you mean? He's an up-and-coming artist, like the rest of you.'

'Huh! He's already got it made!'

'Oh! You mean because of his father being a Count?'

'What? I didn't know about that?'

'Well, he's the younger son, you know. None of the inheritance comes to him. He has to make his own way in life.'

'I should have thought he's already made it.'

'What do you mean?'

'He's famous. Didn't you know? His pictures hang in all the art galleries and in many prestigious houses. Any of his acrylics sell for hundreds of euros, more than that even. Sometimes his work fetches four figures.'

Dani didn't know what to do. Did Lys know? Or was Xavier keeping it secret from her for some reason? The question was, should she tell her? Or was it none of her business? How would she feel, if it were her who was being deceived? She knew she would hate to be the last to find out and, decided she would have to tell her quietly, before someone else did.

There was no opportunity that night. When all the leaflets had been pasted around the island, they made their way back to the windmill where Madame Giraud had prepared soup, breads and pastries for them all.

Lys was in high spirits and Dani didn't want to bring her down to earth with what could be unsettling news. The group had travelled from the Le Château by various means and at the end of the evening, they made their way back, Lys transporting four of them squeezed into her car. Dani bade her goodnight and cycled back to Vertbois.

Alex noticed her quiet air but Dani led him to believe that she was tired from the bill-posting activity, though she managed to give him a lively account of the supper afterwards, dispelling any seeds of worry.

'You've had an exciting day,' he agreed. 'Why don't you have a bath and go straight to bed? I've got a load of paperwork still to get through, so I'd be poor company, anyway.'

Dani agreed and, with only a light kiss, they parted company for the night.

The next morning, after a night of restless concern, Dani knew she had to tell Lys what Marcel had said. Fortunately, Alex was free again that morning and Dani told him she wouldn't be long, just some sorting out she had to do.

Once at the windmill, Dani asked Lys to slip into the craft shop for a minute. Without any ado, she gently told her what Marcel had said, adding, 'I know it's none of my business, but, if Marcel knows, you can bet that others do, too. I thought it had better be me to tell you.'

Lys gaped at her. 'Are you sure?' she faltered. 'He's never said. No. You must be mistaken. It must be someone else.'

Dani raised an eyebrow. 'There's only

one Xavier Monsigny, younger son to Le Comte de Monsigny? He earns commissions in hundreds of euros, thousands, even. Your boyfriend's a celebrity, my dear.'

9

Lys's face changed from bewilderment to anger, and then to a dawning light of understanding.

'No wonder he was upset when three of his paintings were stolen earlier in the year soon after he came here. They were all commissioned paintings. He might have told me. I've probably made such a fool of myself, offering to pay my way and even loan him some money at times.'

Her face fell. 'I feel cheated! Why couldn't he tell me? What difference would it have made? If Marcel knows, I bet everyone else does as well. They're probably all thinking I'm hanging on to him, only after his money.'

Dani could understand her feeling a bit aggrieved but felt she was going too far with it. 'Don't be silly. No-one seeing you together would think any such thing.'

'It's all very well for you to say that! You're not the one they're poking the finger at.'

'And neither are you. You're making . . . '

Lys held out her hand as if warding Dani away. 'No! Don't say any more. I'm going to go and see what he has to say for himself.' Lys swung on her heels and stalked out of the shop before Dani could say any more.

Dani returned to Vertbois in a subdued frame of mine. She was sure it would all blow over, but she didn't like to think of Lys being unhappy. Maybe she should have kept the information to herself.

Alex was busy setting out Christian's wooden railway track on the lounge floor when she returned. He looked up at her. 'Everything all right?' he asked perceptively.

Dani was too upset to tell him about the matter, and wasn't sure Lys would want her to do so anyway.

'Yes, fine,' she replied. 'I just wanted

to check over something with Lys. It's the opening tomorrow. We want everything to go well.'

'Come and see my trains!' Christian called. 'Papa is making a super layout.'

Glad of the diversion, Dani pushed the matter to one side. There was nothing more she could do about it for now, anyway.

They spent a pleasant day together. After Alex had completed some work on his lap-top, that he explained was connected to the main business computer via the internet, they had lunch and then took an excited Christian to St Trojan, where a narrow-gauge railway ran through the forest and sand dunes to the Gatseau beach.

The small train was a picturesque, ancient model, pulling half a dozen open-sided carriages that were almost filled by a party of excited young school children.

'Wow! That must be a nice school to go to!' Christian exclaimed on being told. 'Will the school I go to come to the beach in a train?'

Alex laughed, ruffling his hair. 'I don't suppose they come every day. I expect it's a treat for the end of term. I bet they have to go back to school and write about it.'

Christian still seemed enthralled by the idea and was reluctant to leave the train to go on to the beach. The engine driver let him try his hat on and promised that he would be allowed to stand in his cab before their return journey later on, if he was a good boy and did as his mama and papa were telling him.

Alex and Dani exchanged a secret smile over his head and Alex linked fingers into Dani's as they strolled behind Christian, who was now eager to run over the last dune to see the sea.

To any casual onlookers, they did indeed seem like a normal family group. Dani's heart felt warmed by the thought. She was beginning to wonder why the thought of taking on someone else's child had seemed so terrifying until a short while ago.

Later, after their evening meal, Dani asked if she might make another visit to see Lys. 'Just to make sure everything is ready for tomorrow,' she excused herself. In her own happiness, the thought of Lys's temporary upset with Xavier cast a shadow over everything.

Alex laughed good-naturedly. 'Your evening time is your own,' he reminded her. 'Take the car, if you like.'

Dani wondered what reception she would receive from Lys. When she arrived at the windmill, it was to see Lys, Etienne and a few of the artisans stringing bunting around the car park and making everywhere look bright and festive. She couldn't see Xavier anywhere but waited until everyone else had gone before bringing the question into the open.

Lys pulled a face. 'He's gone up to the northern end of the island, to La Côte Sauvage, Chassiron and St Denis, 'to find some peace and quiet', he said.'

Lys's voice was flat and Dani

immediately put her arms around her. 'He'll be back. He'd said he wanted to go up there, before all this.'

'Yes, but not like this. Not just now. And he said he'd hoped I'd get over my fit of the sulks whilst he was away.'

Dani was sympathetic. 'Not the best of 'au revoirs',' she said wryly. 'What did you say to that?'

'Nothing! Just be glad I didn't have anything in my hand to pour over his head. I felt like it, I can tell you.'

'Oh, poor you, and lucky Xavier! You will make up, though, won't you?' Dani asked lightly, trying to defuse Lys's annoyance. 'After all, what if Xavier had told you straight away? Would it really have made any difference to your feelings for him?'

To her relief, Lys considered the point. 'I don't know. I suppose I'd have felt he was out of my league, socially and financially,' she admitted honestly. 'As it is, I still feel he hasn't trusted me enough to tell me his true status. It was bad enough finding out that his father is a Count, but I still thought he was an up and coming artist, not an already established one making pots of money. I thought we were beginning things together, both building our careers. I'll never be able to earn anything like what Xavier earns from his paintings.'

'So what? Isn't it more important that you love each other?' Dani asked reasonably.

As it was getting late, the two girls bade each other goodnight and Dani drove back to Vertbois in a lighter frame of mind than she had left, feeling sure that when Xavier returned the following day, Lys and he would kiss and make up.

* * *

They all awoke to a beautiful day. The sun was shining but there was enough breeze to make sure that Etienne would get his wish of officially opening his windmill turning the sails and not the new 'highfaluting' electric motor!

Etienne spent the morning making sure that all was as ready as it could be. Madame Giraud was busy in her bakery, producing the last batches of rolls, pastries and cakes, which would be on sale after the ceremony.

Alex, with Christian in tow, helped some of the other willing helpers to adjust the tethering of the gazebos they had bought, and setting out the plastic tables and chairs under their shade, whilst Dani checked that she knew where everything in the craft shop was situated and initiated Suzie, Lys's newly-appointed sales-girl, into their system of sales.

Lys busied herself overseeing everything, and keeping a watchful eye open for Xavier's arrival. She was destined to be disappointed.

By the time the opening ceremony had been conducted by the local mayor, Etienne had released the brake to set the magnificent sails in motion to the accompaniment of shouts and cheers, the visitors had made their tour of the windmill, and all but the crumbs of Madame Giraud's excellent fare had been eaten, Lys had to admit that Xavier wasn't coming.

Her smile was bright, and possibly only Dani and Etienne could see how brittle it was. To her grandfather, Lys excused herself as being uptight about all the arrangements going smoothly and to Dani, she mouthed silently, 'Don't ask!'

Dani kept an anxious, watchful eye on her friend as they all worked together to tidy everything away at the end of the day, but knew better than to try to talk to her about Xavier's non-appearance. She wondered if he had forgotten about it, in view of his difference of opinion with Lys, but didn't think it very likely. Nothing else had been talked about for days and, if the number of uninvited visitors was anything to go by, the whole island knew about it.

Maybe it was her uncertainty over Lys's future relationship with Xavier that, the following day, made Dani more acutely aware of areas of equal uncertainty in her association with Alex.

She had been helping Christian with some jigsaw puzzles and, when he was busy painting a picture of the windmill, she made a cafetiére of coffee and carried a small tray with two mugs on it into Alex's study. He had shown her into it on her first visit but it was the first time she had gone into the room whilst Alex was working on his computer.

Having the tray in her hands, she hadn't been able to knock but had used her elbow to hold down the door handle and pushed the door open with a swing of her hip.

'Morning! Coffee time!' she announced brightly, placing the tray on to the edge of Alex's desk where none of his papers were lying. 'Sorry! Did I make you jump?'

At her unannounced entry, Alex had made a sound of annoyance and immediately blanked his screen with a flick of the mouse.

Dani leaned over his bent shoulders and slipped her arms around his neck, nestling her lips against his cheek, revelling in the aromatic scent of his aftershave.

'Oh, I've not made you lose your work, have I?' she exclaimed in dismay.

'No, but I always tell Christian not to disturb me in here, or to knock if needs must.'

His voice was affable and Dani only felt a mild reproof. She mischievously sat on his lap.

'This isn't getting my work done,' he growled at her, gently flicking her nose.

'No, but it's so much nicer, isn't it?' She grinned.

'My boss won't think so!'

'Who is your boss?' Dani asked curiously. 'What exactly do you do? I mean, I know you said that you manage a team of salesmen, but what do they sell?'

A closed expression flitted across Alex's face, causing Dani to pull back with a start.

'I'm not prying,' she said hastily. 'I just wondered, that's all.'

Alex looked steadily at her face, glanced away and then turned back to her. 'I can't really tell you,' he said slowly, as if considering his words carefully. 'It's not that I don't trust you, it just involves too many risky details. It's better that you don't know.'

Dani frowned. 'Risky? You mean dangerous? To whom? You? Or to others?'

Alex shrugged his shoulders slightly. 'Both. Me, others, maybe even you and Christian. No, not that. I'd never allow that!'

He cupped her chin in his hand. 'I'm seriously thinking of changing my job. But, I can't, not just yet. I've got to finish what I'm involved with right now. It wouldn't be fair to my colleagues to pull out now. But I will, as soon as I can.

'And then will you be able to tell me what it's all about?'

Alex hesitated. 'Maybe. Probably not

all the details, but I'll tell you as much as I can without betraying confidences. Will that do?'

Dani felt slightly disturbed. She couldn't imagine what secrets Alex might have, secrets that could lead him, and possibly Christian and herself, into danger. She thought of the clown outfit that hung in his cupboard and her previous disturbing thoughts about that. Had his light explanation of being a clown in the carnival procession been the truth? The whole truth?

Suddenly, she felt unsure and she slid off his lap before her doubts showed on her face.

'It'll have to, for now,' she murmured lightly. 'I'd better get back to Christian. I've left him on his own long enough.'

10

Alex was already up and dressed when Dani emerged from her room the following morning.

'I've been called away again,' Alex announced with regret in his voice. 'It might even be overnight. Can you cope with that? I hadn't meant to be away so soon but it can't be avoided.'

'The nature of the job,' Dani surmised.

Her remark drew a sharp look from Alex. 'I have to go!'

Dani shrugged. 'Yes. I'm sorry. The details of your job aren't any of my business.'

'I'm hoping they will be. That's why I'm thinking of making this my last operation.'

His voice held a note of appeal and Dani immediately regretted her tone of pique. Alex didn't know how she had spent much of the previous night worrying over many scenarios that were probably more the result of her over-active imagination than based on any facts or commonsense.

She moved towards him and lifted her arms to encircle his neck. Alex's lips immediately sought hers and they kissed each other hungrily. When they parted, Dani, her hands still entwined around Alex's neck, searched his face seriously with her eyes.

'I can't help worrying about you,' she said quietly. 'It's worse not knowing what the dangers are. At least if I knew what you are facing, I could forget about all the other dangers.'

'Like man-eating tigers and getting drowned in the rapids?'

At least it made her laugh and defused the tension. 'Anyway, off you go! I'll see to Christian. We'll probably go to the beach again this morning, whilst it's still cool. I was going to ask if I could nip over to speak to Lys, but I'll phone her instead.'

'Is there a problem there?' Alex was picking up his car keys and his attaché case as he spoke.

'Not really. Didn't you notice that Xavier missed the opening ceremony yesterday? He hasn't been in touch since they had a little . . . not exactly a row . . . more a difference of opinion, the previous day, and he's taken himself off.'

Alex's eyes flickered with interest. 'Has he left the island?'

Dani wondered why his interest was so sharp. 'No, not as far as we know. He said he was going off to the northern end of the island, ostensibly to get some different sketches. It's probably all and nothing, but I just thought I'd like to know if he's been in touch this morning.'

Her answer seemed to dispel Alex's surprising concern and he leaned forwards to kiss her lips. 'As you say, you can phone Lys instead. Let me know how they got on, though I'm sure everything will be all right.'

Christian suddenly appeared, still in his pyjamas. 'Are you going away again, Papa?'

'Yes. Be a good boy for Dani. I hope to be back tomorrow.'

After breakfast, she phoned Lys and she could tell at once by the happier tome of Lys's voice, that Xavier had been in touch.

'There was a text message on my phone when I looked,' Lys confessed with a laugh. 'Apparently, one of the paintings that was stolen from his studio after he came here has been seen in a house on the mainland near Poitiers, and the police asked him to go along with them to formally identify it.'

For some unknown reason, the mention that Xavier had left the island brought back to Dani's memory Alex's unexplained interest in his whereabouts, but she dismissed the notion as nonsensical. She was imagining an interest where there had only been polite enquiry, she was sure.

After a few more comments about

the previous day's ceremony, Dani ended the call and gave her full attention to Christian's needs.

Their day went as planned. The morning on the beach, digging another sandcastle, paddling and jumping in the sea and gathering some small clams to make into a simple risotto for their main meal later on in the day.

Christian helped to winkle out the tiny creatures from their shells after they had been cooked in a pan of water for a few minutes and watched with interest as she prepared the rest of the ingredients in preparation for later.

'When Papa makes a risotto, it comes out of a packet!' Christian exclaimed. 'I didn't know you could make it like this. It is more, more, healthier like this?'

It wasn't a hard job to care for him and she was finding him more and more endearing as each day passed, and, even though it was only her second day living in with Alex and Christian, she felt so much at home as to believe that there was no foundation to her fears that she wouldn't be able to manage to take a full place in the small family. If only she didn't have so many niggling doubts about Alex's job.

What were its dangers? And why should those dangers be threatening to Christian and herself? They didn't even know what Alex did, and never came into contact with any part of his work, except by seeing him at work on his computer. And even that was behind a closed door.

It was altogether too mystifying.

Again as planned, after a light lunch of sandwiches and small salad, Dani took Christian into the forest that bordered the coastal dunes. There were walking paths and wider, sandy tracks for equestrian use criss-crossing the forest and there was no danger of getting lost in it as the sea bordered one side to the west and a coastal lane ran parallel along the other edge.

It was cool beneath the shade of the branches and Christian happily ran hither and thither collecting large pinecones and dropping them into Dani's sack. She knew they would add a distinctive flavour to the food cooked on the barbecue she hoped they would have the following day, if Alex had returned by then. If not, they would keep until he was back again, and Dani was determined not to worry any more about his whereabouts. And certainly not to become a nagging girlfriend.

Back at the house, Christian asked if he could watch a video whilst Dani was getting their meal ready.

'You know how to put it on, don't you?' she asked, having seen him insert and play a video on one of her previous visits. 'Which are you choosing?'

'*Bob The Builder*. The one where they move all the sand.'

She smiled, making her way into the kitchen. She was glad she'd done all the preparation earlier. The warmth of the day had taken its toll and she felt tired enough to be thankful of the chance of an early night.

She realised that Christian was

calling something to her and, wiping her hands on a hand-towel, she went through to the lounge.

'It's bad men again!' Christian told her. 'Look! More guns going bang-bang!'

Dani sighed in exasperation and frowned at him. 'You know Papa doesn't like you watching the news programme, Christian. Switch over to the video programme, like you said you would, there's a good boy.'

'No clowns, this time,' Christian remarked, moving towards the television set and reaching out his hand to switch over the programme.

'Wait a minute, Christian!' Dani said sharply. 'Leave it a moment!'

Her ears had picked up the name of the town where the shoot-out was taking place. It was Poitiers. Wasn't that where Xavier had gone yesterday?

The commentator was speaking of a daring raid by a gang of criminals on a large country home, a beautiful chateau set in lovely grounds. Apparently, tipped off by an informant, the police had been lying in wait for the thieves, but the under-cover operation had gone wrong when hostages were taken and part of the armed gang had barricaded themselves and the hostages in an unassailable part of the building.

A couple of police officers and maybe one of the armed raiders had been injured during the shoot-out, and at least two of the gang had managed to get away in a stolen vehicle. Mention was made of other such unresolved raids in the previous few months and the possibility of a link between this raid and those carried out by a gang dressed as clowns was being considered.

Dani's blood ran cold. She gripped the back of the nearest chair and took a few deep breaths. There was only speculation about the connection. There was absolutely no need for her imagination to run riot again, simply because an eager young newscaster wanted to inject a bit of spice of intrigue and conspiracy into what might have been a humdrum stalemate.

Even so, she couldn't help feeling more than a little disturbed.

'Are the clowns there again, Dani?' Christian asked anxiously.

'No, dear. The newsreader is only thinking they might be. You can't see any clowns; can you?'

'No.'

'There you are, then. Now, switch over to the video programme and I'll get on with our meal. The rice is already cooked, so it won't take long. I'll call you when it's ready.'

Dani watched Christian switch over to his video programme and left him to it. As she passed by the foot of the stairs, she paused, the vision of the clown's outfit bright in her mind.

It would be there. She knew it would. There was no point in going to look.

Even so, she slowly made her way upstairs. She wasn't proud of herself. What little faith she had in the man she thought she loved enough to marry him and become the step-mother of his son.

Nevertheless, now she was here, she may as well prove to herself just how unworthy was her suspicion!

She swiftly crossed over to the cupboard and pulled open the door.

The clown's outfit wasn't there . . .

She opened the next door, and the next. She rifled through drawer after drawer, but the clown's outfit had clearly been removed and she knew without doubt that, even though it hadn't been mentioned as being used during the raid, it had been taken there in case it were needed.

She sank on to the edge of a chair and dropped her head into her hands.

Why was Alex mixed up in such a despicable series of crime? Surely he had so much more about him that he could have chosen from any number of occupations and careers. How could she love such a man?

Did she still love him?

Her heart felt deeply sad and heavy, but it was impossible to fall out of love as quickly as that. Maybe, over time, she would bring herself to forget him, but, right now, she still loved him with an intensity that stabbed like a knife deep within her.

What was she do? Could she bear to continue to live in his house? To take care of his son? Another wrench of pain twisted inside her. She loved Christian. It wasn't his fault that his father was a hardened criminal.

Oh, he'd said he was thinking of dropping out of the gang, but that was probably only talk.

No wonder he had spoken of danger to himself, and to her and Christian.

They would be in very deep danger if there were any fear of the likelihood of Alex turning informer.

What was she to do?

Without the complication of having to take care of Christian until Alex's return, she might have decided to pack her things and walk out of Alex's life right there and then, but she couldn't do that. Christian needed her.

And what if Alex were among the

injured ones? Who would take care of Christian then?

With despair in her heart, she couldn't do the sensible thing and leave there and then. Neither could she plan to leave until Alex was home again. She had to face him and tell him of her discovery, and then take her leave of him, however painful it might be.

Still stunned, she sat immobile for a few more minutes, until she recalled that she was in the process of making Christian's meal. She woodenly tidied the clothes she had rummaged through in Alex's cupboard and returned to the kitchen, moving purely on automatic pilot.

She did her best to act normally when she called Christian to the kitchen to eat his meal, unable to face having any of it herself. Her throat felt constricted and she knew she would be unable to swallow.

Fortunately, Christian was full of the excitement of his video and beyond asking her why she wasn't eating and receiving her answer with childhood acceptance, he seemed unaware that anything was amiss.

'Can I watch some more before my bath time?' he asked. 'I'll be very quick getting ready for bed.'

She was thankful to let him. It postponed the time when she would be on her own with nothing to dispel the sense of hopelessness that filled her heart.

She heard the doorbell ring and called out to Christian, 'I'll get it, Christian!'

Maybe it was Lys? Should she tell her friend of her growing fears about Alex's so-called job? A problem shared was a problem halved, wasn't it?

She undid the door, and leapt back as it was thrust inwards towards her, pressing her against the cottage wall.

Two figures rushed inside. She assumed they were men by their strength and build but it was impossible to be sure as they were dressed as clowns.

'Grab hold of her!' the leading one snapped, rushing past into the lounge. 'I'll get the kid!'

'No! No! You mustn't!' Dani shouted, trying to follow after him.

Her arms were cruelly twisted behind her back and she was held in a grip of steel.

'Shut up!' her captor hissed in her ear.

She heard a shout and a cry from Christian and tried to wriggle free but it was no use.

The other clown appeared in the doorway of the lounge, half-dragging, half-carrying a screaming and wriggling Christian in his powerful grasp.

'Dani! Dani!' Christian screamed. 'Where's my Papa?'

'I don't know, love. Why are you doing this?' she shouted at the men. 'Who are you? What do you want?'

'Never you mind!' the one holding Christian snarled at her. 'Just tell his 'Papa',' said in sneering tones, 'that if he doesn't get his men off the job, he won't see his son ever again!'

He pushed past her and her captor, dragging Christian with him, a hand over his mouth in an attempt to stifle his screams. The man holding her thrust away from her and made to follow his accomplice.

They were getting away and taking Christian with them!

Dani regained her balance and dashed after the men. Their progress was hindered by Christian's struggles and she caught up with them at the gate.

'You can't do this to a child!' she begged. 'Take me instead. Alex will want to get me back.'

She still couldn't sort out in her mind what was happening and what part Alex played in it. Was this a tiff among gangs? Had they discovered that he wanted to get out?

She clung on to the man's arm, dodging the blows he aimed at her head.

'We need the boy!' the man in front

snarled, giving Christian a vicious shake.

'Then take me, too.' Dani begged. 'Let me come with him. He'll be so frightened on his own.'

They were through the gate and Christian was already being thrust headfirst into the car. Dani screamed, hoping Madame Toussaint would hear and phone for help.

The leading clown seemed to be aware of the likelihood of attention being drawn to their kidnap attempt.

Dani was hustled on to the back seat of the car, almost on top of Christian and, as the second clown fell in on top of her, the car surged forward in reckless motion.

11

Alex froze when his extra-alert senses told him that someone was approaching his position. He was lying at full-length on the ground, his eyes never wavering from the gun-sights of his high-powered rifle. He knew his back was covered and, when someone tapped him on the shoulder, he half-turned his head.

'What is it, Hervé?'

Hervé, like himself, was flat on the ground and had approached him by wriggling forwards on his bent elbows and splayed-out knees.

'I've been told to relieve you. Something's come up.'

Alex grunted in annoyance. 'It had better be good!'

He'd been in the game too long to ignore a peremptory order; he left that to impetuous hotheads and over-confident firebrands, and usually found that they didn't last long.

It was his ability to keep cool under fire that had taken him along the fast-track as far as it had, and had been the reason that he hadn't pulled out before now, even though Trudi had begged him to do so after Christian was born. After Trudi's untimely death, he had no longer wanted to pull out and, for a couple of months, had almost become as reckless as those he scorned. However, this was going to be his final operation and he didn't want to leave it only half-done.

He wriggled backwards until he knew he was through the bushes and out of sight of enemy-fire. Then, in a fluid movement, he drew up his knees, twisted his body and sprang to his feet into a semi-crouched position.

A similarly crouched figure a few metres away beckoned him to follow and, at a crouched half-run, the two men swiftly covered a few more metres. It was Alex who called a halt to the retreat.

'This is far enough! What's happened?'

'Bad news, I'm afraid. There's been some sort of a raid on your house, and there's no sign of your son and whoever you had with him.'

Alex's heart momentarily stopped beating and a cold shaft struck his middle. 'Any sign of violence?'

'A bit of disturbance in the living room, and the door left wide open. And deep tyre marks in the gravel outside by the gate suggesting a quick get-away.'

'Any blood?'

'No.'

'Right! Who's in charge of the incident?'

'The local gendarmerie. They've searched the house and set up a watch, but I don't think they expect anyone to return there. They've got what they went for.'

'And no word yet from the perpetrators? No bargaining plea?'

'No. They'll be covering their tracks

before they do that. They'll be somewhere on the mainland by now. No knowing where.'

Alex was silent, his mind working overtime. It was something he had dreaded happening but hadn't really thought ever would. He'd thought a non-descript house on Ile d'Oléron a safe enough place. He'd underestimated his foes.

'Right. Let me know the minute anything comes in.'

He felt helpless. There was nothing he could do, except get back to his post and do the job he was trained to do.

Dani held Christian tightly to her chest. His hysterical sobs had quietened now and his body just convulsed every so often as he choked back on a sob.

The car had darkened windows and, although she had tried to see something of the outside world, she could only glimpse a faded scenario. They were off the island, she knew that, there had been no mistaking the structure of the viaduct as they passed over it.

Now they were passing through flat countryside with trees bordering the roadside but with very little else to distinguish one area from another, and she didn't know the Charente Maritime area well enough to hazard a guess.

She burrowed her face into Christian's hair and swallowed hard. What was going to happen to them? Did Alex know yet? And what could he do, if he did?

Christian seemed to sense her disquiet. 'Dani,' he whispered, lifting his face slightly. 'I'm scared.'

Dani nuzzled her lips against his hair and forehead. 'It'll be all right, Christian. Papa will get us free.'

'He'd better!' growled the clown at her side.

'Quit talking!' the driver snapped. 'This is no game we're playing.'

Eventually, Dani knew they were on the autoroute by the speed of the vehicle and, at some point, she realised the driver was talking into his mobile phone. His words chilled her and she was glad that Christian had fallen asleep.

Dani tried to move her position slightly.

'Don't move!' the man beside her snapped.

'My arm's hurting,' she protested quietly.

'Be glad you can feel it! You'll feel nothing when you're dead.'

Dani tried to relax to ease the pain. She had to keep her wits about her. These men were jumpy and unpredictable. She didn't want to spook them into more violence.

Some time later, their speed lessened and she knew they were on the ordinary roads. The going roughened beneath them and after a kilometre or so, the car drew to a halt in a wooded area. It was very dark and, once the car's headlights had been switched off, they were in pitch darkness.

The driver got out. She heard what she thought to be the safety catch of a gun being released. The door at her side was wrenched open.

'Get out!'

Dani's heart thudded. Christian's weight lay heavy on her and she knew she couldn't lift him.

'Christian's asleep,' she objected.

'So what? My heart bleeds for him! Get him out!'

Dani shook him gently and, somehow, the half-awake child managed to stumble along at her side the short distance to the dark shape of a single-storey dwelling that loomed out in front of them. The man in front kicked open the door and the other man hustled them inside.

Dani lost her footing and fell forward, taking Christian down with her. Christian began to cry and Dani hugged him to her.

'It's all right! It's all right!' she urged him to believe, although she didn't believe it herself. She tried to scramble to her feet but one of the men thrust her back again onto the hard, cold ground.

'Stay where you are!' he commanded.

Oh, Alex, where are you? We need you. And, although she didn't know what part Alex was playing in all this, she knew definitely now that she loved him and that nothing would be right until she had told him so.

* * *

It was a long night for those on watch outside the château. Arc lights had been set up the previous evening before daylight had completely faded and a constant watch had been maintained.

The first direct contact from the kidnappers had come just before the end of Alex's first watch and the message had been passed on immediately. It merely confirmed his and everyone else's expectations. Christian's release was dependent on their immediate and complete withdrawal.

'Did they get a fix on their position?' Alex wanted to know.

'Not quite. They were using a mobile

phone, probably on the autoroute. We lost contact, so they probably switched off. We'll be ready for their next call and, once we get a definite fix on a vehicle, we'll get the helicopter on their trail.'

By morning, Lys was in a state of anxiety.

Throughout the previous evening she had attempted to get in touch with both Xavier and Dani. Xavier's mobile was listed as being unavailable, he must have switched it off and forgotten to switch it back on, and Dani's phone simply rang on and on. Wherever she was, she hadn't taken her phone with her.

They had had a busy day at the windmill and tidying up had taken longer than usual. Lys tried to push her anxieties out of her mind. What was there to worry about?

However, when the same thing happened at her repeated attempts the next day, she left her grandfather in charge of affairs at the windmill and drove the short distance to Vertbois.

She wasn't entirely sure which house Alex had rented for the summer but her memory of Dani's words made her think it was on a road on the left as you approached the village just before the first crossroad and that was where she turned.

The sight of a guard of gendarmes outside one of the houses added to her apprehension. She drove past. After all, there were a number of pretty side roads where the residence could be, but as soon as she saw a place to turn around, she did so, and retraced her way.

She hesitated as she got out of her car. She was probably about to make a fool of herself, but she had to risk it.

Her fears were well founded. When she asked if that were the house rented by Alex Gallepe, the gendarme on duty didn't deny it. He was careful not to betray any information, but suggested that she went to the local gendarmerie and asked her questions there.

Now extremely anxious, she did as she was bidden.

Her reasons for enquiry were asked for and given and, eventually, when she had answered all of their questions, she was given the information that Mademoiselle Cachart and Christian Gallepe were being regarded as missing persons but that nothing more could be said.

'But where's Alex? Doesn't he know where they are? I'd like to see him, if you don't mind! Tell him it's Lys, Dani's friend. He knows who I am.'

'I'm afraid Monsieur Gallepe is also unavailable, mademoiselle. We have your contact address and phone number. That is all we can say at the moment.'

With faint hope of any success, she went into the newsagent's shop and picked up a daily newspaper. The headline shocked her almost insensible. Holding her breath, she read on, reading more or less what Dani had heard on the previous night's early news programme.

What leaped out and hit Lys in the

eye was the added fact that one of the hostages at the siege of the château was believed to be Xavier Monsigny, the brilliant young artist, son of Count de Monsigny.

She bought the paper, staggered outside and sat on a seat in the square where she read the whole article again, unable to take it all in. Xavier had gone to Poitiers to identify one of his stolen paintings. How had he come to be caught up in the foiled robbery?

It was quite a while later that she remembered that Dani was missing also, but couldn't see any possible connection between her disappearance and Xavier's risky position.

How could she find out more? They didn't have television at the windmill cottage. The tabac! That was the place!

She almost wished she hadn't gone there when the late-morning news came on with its live bulletin of the current stage of the siege. Diversionary tactics were being employed and a great deal of smoke was pouring out from the rear of the château and some gunfire could be heard from some unidentified quarters.

When there was a sudden rush in through the front entrance, Lys found that she was holding her breath. It was all very well for the impersonal voice of the reporter to talk about the extreme bravery of the armed forces involved and that they had been highly trained to shoot to kill, but he didn't have someone he loved on the inside, and the bullets didn't know the difference between the 'good' and the 'bad', did they!

The camera zoomed in through the open front door, just as a small group of people were emerging out of its darkened interior. One man, surrounded by police officers in bullet-proof body jackets, was obviously handcuffed and another must have been injured in some way because he was on a hastily summoned stretcher.

Just as Lys was taking in the fact that his head and body were completely covered by the blanket thrown over him, the newscaster murmured, 'Unfortunately, it seems that Monsieur Monsigny was caught in the crossfire and unconfirmed reports are that he is dead.'

Lys, who had never fainted before in all her life, slid slowly off her stool and crumpled in a heap on the floor.

* * *

Dani and Christian were cold and their limbs stiff. They had been given nothing to eat or drink, and the morning had dragged on interminably. One of their captors, incongruous now in his clown's outfit, had stepped outside to make numerous phone calls and was becoming more and more edgy as the morning progressed.

The one who seemed to be in control of the affair had stepped outside once more with the intention of making yet another call, when a sudden round of gunfire rent the air.

Their guard dived to the floor,

rasping, 'Don't move or I'll shoot!' over his shoulder. He pulled a gun out of his belt and waved it in Dani's direction.

For a moment, Dani froze.

Christian began to whimper and Dani drew him towards her, holding him closely to her, hoping he wouldn't panic.

A metallic high-powered voice boomed into the silence of the wood, magnified by a megaphone.

'We have you completely surrounded. Come out with your hands in the air and we'll hold our fire.'

The man was clearly panicked. His eyes darted around the room, as if looking for inspiration for his next move.

'I think you'd better do as they say,' Dani said quietly, trying to keep her voice from shaking. 'They've obviously got your friend.'

'Shut up! I've got to think!'

He waved the gun towards Christian. 'You, boy, come here!'

Christian shrank even further into

Dani's side and she clasped her hands around him, half-turning her body away from the man as he rose to his feet, to shield Christian from the threat of his gun.

'Fetch him here!'

He lumbered towards them, the hand holding the gun swinging from side to side.

Dani hugged Christian tighter, unable to even contemplate letting the man get anywhere near him.

'Get out of here!' she screamed at him.

She stood up, her face like that of an angry tigress. She thrust Christian behind her and leapt at the man, her hands like claws in front of her. She didn't even think of the danger she was putting herself in. She heard the sound of a loud bang very close to her head and a scream from Christian.

The scream fired her anger even more and she flung herself bodily at the man, her hands clawing at his face. Her onslaught made the man stagger backwards, almost losing his balance.

Behind her, the door of the cottage crashed open and suddenly the cottage seemed full of men shouting, barking orders, the sheer force of their entrance overpowering.

She knew she was falling and couldn't stop herself and she collapsed in a crumpled heap on the hard ground.

12

It was nearly a week later when Dani heard the full story. In between times, she had been aware of a succession of hazy events. There had been a rushed journey to hospital, sirens blaring, and she heard Christian's voice crying, 'Don't die, Dani.'

Somehow, she knew she was in Alex's arms and he was murmuring, 'I love you, Dani. Stay with us! Stay with us!'

The next she knew, she was lying in bed. Alex's face was looking down at her and he was smiling. His face kept going in and out of focus and she wondered how he did that.

'You crazy, mad girl,' he said, his tone belying his words. 'You could have been killed.'

'He wanted Christian,' she managed to whisper through dry lips. 'I couldn't let him.'

Alex took hold of her hand. A pain, deep in her shoulder, made her wince but she was glad he didn't let go.

'I thought I was losing both of you,' Alex said softly. 'I'd have had nothing left to live for.'

A while later, Alex was holding Christian up so that he could see her, his face white and anxious.

'Are you all right, Dani?' he asked.

She smiled at him. 'Yes, love. I'm fine.'

'That's good. Those nasty clowns have gone now. Papa says they won't come back.'

Dani nodded. She was tired and wanted to sleep.

Another time, Lys was there, her face streaked with tears but when Dani asked what the matter was, Lys just said, 'Nothing. Just get better for us. Grandpère sends his love.'

And then her parents were there, her mother tearful but smiling bravely and her father looking a little strained but managing a hearty smile.

Each day was better than the last and, when at last she was able to sit propped up on pillows so that she could see her visitors properly, she asked, 'Is someone going to tell me what it was all about?'

They were all there, all the ones who mattered, and she glanced round them all, but her eyes finally rested on Alex.

'It was all tied up with my work,' he began. 'I wasn't able to tell you what I did because I am an undercover police agent. Our main current job was to investigate a series of bank raids and other daring thefts in various large houses and chateaux, and we knew that Lys's boyfriend, Xavier Monsigny, was related to one of the suspects, his brother, Henri.'

Dani nodded. She looked at Lys. 'You told me Xavier thought he had had something to do with the theft of his paintings, didn't you? Had he?'

Lys nodded but it was Alex that continued.

'Yes, and one of the paintings had

come to light when someone approached a known collector of Xavier's work. He knew about its theft and he told the man he was interested but needed to think about it and arrange to have the painting verified. He then got in touch with us and we arranged to be present when they brought it back to his chateau. We needed Xavier there to identify it.'

'That's where he had gone, when he went missing,' Lys put in.

Dani nodded but turned her eyes back to Alex, who was continuing his tale.

'However, things went slightly wrong when Henri himself turned up with the painting. He, of course, recognised his brother immediately and realised that something had gone amiss. He grabbed hold of Xavier, using him as a body-shield. They had more men than we had anticipated because, it transpired, they were using the painting as a way to get inside the chateau in order to rob it, not just to sell the painting.

'In the ensuing gun battle, two policemen were injured and Henri and three others, with Xavier as hostage, managed to hole themselves up in a wing of the chateau. Two others, who weren't involved in the gun battle, got away and kidnapped you and Christian, hoping that we would immediately call off the siege in return for his safety. He was a wily customer, Henri Monsigny, and, knowing I was heading the investigation, had already discovered where Christian and I were living.'

'Was?' Dani queried, picking up on the past tense of the verb.

'Yes. Unfortunately, he was killed in the final assault.' Alex glanced over to where Xavier was standing with his arm around Lys.

Lys smiled ruefully. 'And I was watching it on television in the tabac in Le Château, and thought it was Xavier who had been killed.'

'Oh! I'm sorry about your brother, Xavier,' Dani said sadly.

Xavier shrugged lightly. 'Yes. It is sad.

But that was the life he lived, drugs, guns, gang warfare.'

Everyone was silent for a moment, thinking of the incident and Dani noticed that Lys clung to him more closely, as if afraid that even now he might be taken from her.

'But how did you find out where we were?' Dani asked Alex.

'Madame Toussaint heard the commotion, so it wasn't very long before we knew you had been taken. They used their mobile phones to each other and to contact us, so we were able to fix on your position, and as soon as it was all over at the château we closed in.

'We hadn't been there long when one of the men came outside. He was that startled after our warning shot, he didn't put up any resistance, then we moved in closer. We were hampered by not knowing exactly where you were in the cottage, so we didn't dare start shooting.

'Then, we heard you yell something and heard a shot, and Christian screamed. We knew it was then or never, so we barged in.'

Christian had climbed unnoticed on to Dani's bed and he now cuddled into her.

'If Papa really had lost you, I'd have found you again,' he told her. 'I want you to live with us always and be my new mama, then we'll never lose you. Will you do that?'

Everyone laughed and Alex stood up and swung Christian off the bed.

'I'll do my own proposing, young man!' He laughed.

'But you will, won't you, Dani?' Christian insisted.

Dani looked from father to son. They were both looking at her expectantly . . . and so was everyone else!

She knew she should make Christian wait for his answer, but there was no doubt in her heart what it would be. She already loved him as dearly as if he were her own.

'Yes, I will, Christian.' She smiled.

She looked at Alex's beaming face

and smiled happily at him. He sat on the edge of her bed with Christian on his knee and leaned forward to kiss her lips.

Dani glared around at everyone else, happy to see the delight in their eyes.

Alex's eyes gleamed.

Love was spinning in the air with the windmill's sails and her heart was reluctant no more.

THE END

Other titles in the
Linford Romance Library:

JUST A SUMMER ROMANCE

Karen Abbott

When Lysette Dupont decides to help her grandfather restore his old windmill on Ile d'Oléron off the west coast of France, she doesn't want to get sidetracked into pursuing a deepening interest in the bohemian artist Xavier Monsigny. Xavier has planned to spend his time on the island painting and sketching — but intrigue and danger draw them into a summer romance . . . for, surely, that is all it will be?

A FAMILY SECRET

Jo James

Symons Hill is a charming, close-knit Australian town, where April Stewart's happiness is linked to Symon Andrews of the area's pioneering family. When he leaves suddenly for the city, rumours abound. Heart-broken, April immerses herself in her animal refuge work until he returns unexpectedly. Though he reawakens her feelings, his actions threaten to change the relaxed character of Symons Hill. What has happened to change this once warm, thoughtful man, and how will April learn the truth?

BECAUSE OF YOU

Catherine Brant

Kay Ballard, a primary school teacher, obtained a position as companion to the children of Simon Nash, the composer. But at Ashleigh, Kay discovered that the composer's home and background were surrounded by mystery. Three years earlier Simon Nash's wife had died in peculiar circumstances, out of which rumour had sprung and flourished . . . How much of the rumour was false, and how much based on fact, became an obsession with Kay. And when the mystery was explained, danger and tragedy were in the air once more.

STAR ATTRACTION

Angela Dracup

To be on tour with Leon Ferrar should be a dream come true, but for Suzy Grey, his assistant, it becomes a nightmare when she finds herself in love with him. Leon is surrounded by beautiful women, from the voluptuous Toni Wells to pianist Angelina Frascana. Leon and Angelina draw close together as they prepare for a concert in Vienna, but Suzy's desperate course of action threatens to ruin her own relationship with Leon for ever.

GLENALLYN'S BRIDE

Mary Cummins

Queen Johanna destroyed the House of Frazer at Dundallon, after the murder of James I. Innes Frazer, step-sister to Sir Archibald, escaped but was captured by a band of beggars. The leader of the beggars, Ruari Stewart, offers her as a bride to Glenallyn. Innes refuses, only to become a servant of the Queen at Edinburgh Castle, where she again meets James Livingstone who was responsible for slaughtering the Frazers. Innes knows that she must find Ruari Stewart, and one day she might become Glenallyn's bride.